By the silver light of the full moon...
Micaela entered her secret garden.

She'd given Kurt a chance to come to her freely. She was tired of waiting.

Tonight she would remove all obstacles from her path. It was midnight, the time when it was easiest to call on the unseen.

She stepped into the very center of the circle of night-blooming flowers and let her green wool cloak fall to the ground. She raised her bare arms to the night sky—and summoned the darkness to do her will.

She took Kurt's leather choker, the one she had stolen from his room. She ran her finger along the leather, feeling the warmth of Kurt's skin.

Holding the choker in one hand, she knelt down and dug a hole in the earth. Gently, she set the choker in it, then planted one of the Hearts of Darkness seedlings over it.

"May his heart grow in love for me as these Hearts of Darkness grow," she chanted. "Let him love me—and no other."

It's written in the stars!
Watch for these Zodiac Chillers in your future…

ZODIAC CHILLER #4
TWISTED TAURUS

by Ellen Steiber

Random House Sprinters
Random House • New York

to Mimi Panitch, who thought it was a great idea
and read Micaela's chart for me

and with thanks to Ruth Koeppel for incredible patience and
inspired editing; Valerie Smith for the horoscopes;
Charlie Goldberg, M.D., and Barb Drye, M.D., for medical
information and music; and Howard Bessen, M.D., for more
medical info—especially the foxglove–van Gogh connection

A RANDOM HOUSE SPRINTER™ PUBLISHED BY RANDOM HOUSE, INC.

Text copyright © 1995 by Ellen Steiber
Cover art copyright © 1995 by Bill Schmidt

Library of Congress Catalog Card Number: 95-075564
ISBN: 0-679-87307-4
RL: 6.5-7.0
First Sprinter edition: October 1995

Manufactured in the United States of America

10 9 8 7 6 5 4 3 2

ZODIAC CHILLERS is a trademark of Random House, Inc.

PROLOGUE

Micaela James walked out of Northridge High, her mind on her dreams.

That morning, just before she'd woken, she'd dreamed the voice again. It was the same voice she'd heard years ago that told her she was an artist. The same voice that guided her to plant her secret garden. The message it gave her that morning was not nearly as clear. But it echoed something she'd been seeing in her horoscopes and in her tarot readings:

The time of isolation is over. Two strangers, a brother and sister, will enter your life and change everything.

Then today in English class, Micaela had heard someone talking about a brother and sister who'd just transferred into Northridge: Kurt and Darci Callahan.

Normally, Micaela didn't pay attention to school gossip. She really didn't care who transferred in or out of Northridge. Aliens could have beamed down into her physics class, and she wouldn't have noticed. But everyone was saying that Kurt was a doll. Smart, good-looking, and hot. Even though school had only been open for a week, Kurt was already being talked about more than any other senior guy. Micaela considered most guys in Northridge a total bore, so she was curious to see whether Kurt Callahan could possibly be different. And the fact that he had a younger sister was too much of a coincidence to ignore.

Now she watched him coming out of school. He was tall and lanky with longish sandy blond hair and cool gray eyes. He wore a gray shirt and skinny black jeans and a leather thong around his neck with a single oblong black glass bead. Another leather thong was tied around his left wrist. He looked like a rock star. A short, dark-haired girl walked beside him. He was looking down at her, and they were both laughing.

Micaela wondered if the girl was his sister. No, she decided, they didn't look anything alike. A girlfriend? Already? Micaela decided to find out.

She watched as they got into an ancient white

VW van. It was definitely his, she decided even before he got in on the driver's side. She got into her own Acura and followed them out of the parking lot.

Ten minutes later the white van parked in front of the Sandy Park Diner. Micaela pulled in after it and watched as Kurt and the girl went inside. After a few moments she followed them. They were sitting in a booth near the back of the diner, studying the menus. Micaela took the booth behind them.

And listened.

"So what are you having?" Kurt asked.

"You treating?" the girl said.

"Dream on," he answered. "I'm your brother, not your date."

So they *were* brother and sister.

"Then I'll have a chocolate shake and fries," Darci decided.

"You are *so* predictable," Kurt teased her. "Isn't this the same girl who told me she was going to be a new person when we moved to Northridge? Something about losing five pounds?"

"Oh, shut up," Darci said with a smile as the waitress came to take their orders.

"So," Kurt said as the waitress moved on to Micaela's table, "how's it going so far?"

"Great," Darci answered.

"The truth," her brother insisted gently. "I saw you today when you came out of gym class. You looked like you wanted to be anywhere else on the planet but there."

Darci sighed heavily. "You want the truth? I haven't made a single friend yet. The sophomore class is super-tight—they've all been in the same cliques since the seventh grade. No one even talks to me."

"It's only the first week of school," Kurt said. "Give it time. Things will open up for you. You'll make the connections you want. Before you know it, you'll probably be best friends with someone very mysterious and exotic."

"Is that a promise?" Darci asked skeptically.

"I'll treat you to a dinner next time if I'm wrong," Kurt vowed.

"You're on," Darci said, sounding more cheerful. "So who's that gorgeous redhead you've got your eye on?"

Micaela sipped at the herbal tea she'd ordered. She liked Kurt and Darci. She liked the way they obviously cared about each other, the way they were not only siblings but friends.

They had to be the brother and sister in her dream. For such a long time now she'd been on her own. She hadn't wanted or needed friends. She'd needed the isolation. It was the only way she could learn the skills she'd acquired. But now it was time for the isolation to end. She was entering a new phase of her life, one in which she was meant to connect with two chosen people. The stars, the tarot—and now the voice—had told her so. And they were never wrong.

Kurt Callahan was going to fall in love with her, and Darci was going to become her best friend. It was as inevitable as the waxing of the moon.

CHAPTER 1

"Feel the earth beneath your hands," Ms. Yarnell told her art class. "Let the earth speak to you. If you listen to the earth, it will guide you."

Darci Callahan squinted at the "earth" beneath her hands, and waited for it to speak. The clay was decidedly silent. *This is so absurd,* Darci thought. She'd been enjoying art class until Ms. Yarnell suddenly decided that the class needed to sculpt. So for the last week Darci had been trying to sculpt a sleeping cat. She'd chosen a cat because it was the easiest thing she could think of that wasn't an ashtray. She squinted at the clay again. No, she wasn't imagining it. Her sleeping cat looked like a plump sausage with ears.

"Clay is a gift of the earth," Ms. Yarnell went on in theatrical tones. "Your sculpture is the earth's voice given form."

Darci rolled her eyes and decided that Ms. Yarnell was a flake. Then again, maybe it was just end-of-the-day syndrome. Darci had noticed that a lot of teachers seemed to come unglued during last period. Although this was Darci's fifth week at Northridge High, she was still getting her bearings. She still wasn't quite sure which teachers were cool and which were losing it. Or who was scum and who was relatively human. She still hadn't made her first real friend.

The girl beside Darci, a senior named Stacey, caught her bewildered glance and grinned. "Ignore it," she whispered. "Ms. Y. goes kind of overboard when she teaches sculpture. I think the smell of the clay affects her brain—all of a sudden she thinks she's an earth goddess or something."

Darci grinned back. "Thanks for the warning."

"Darci." Ms. Yarnell suddenly materialized directly in front of her. "I don't think you're feeling the clay."

"It just feels kind of cold and damp to me," Darci said honestly.

Ms. Yarnell closed her eyes. "Become one with the clay," she said in a hushed voice.

Darci wished her brother Kurt were here. Kurt would be rolling on the floor, laughing. Then again, Kurt wasn't the type to take art classes.

Darci sighed with relief as Ms. Yarnell moved on to critique another student. She picked up her clay, held it in one hand, then the other. Nada. This piece of earth was definitely not communicating. With a sigh, Darci mushed her cat back into a lump.

Stacey nudged her. "You've got to see what Micaela is sculpting," she whispered. "It's so good, it's scary."

"Who's Micaela?" Darci asked.

Stacey gestured toward the other side of the room. "Micaela James," she said. "The girl in the green shirt."

Darci glanced up and saw a tall, slender girl wearing a soft pale green shirt over faded jeans. Her long white-blond hair was pinned loosely to the top of her head with silver combs. A few wavy tendrils clung to the back of her neck. Her sleeves were rolled to just above her elbows, and she wore a mass of silver bangles on each wrist. She seemed completely absorbed in her work.

Darci stood on tiptoe to peer over the other students—but she couldn't tell what it was that Micaela was sculpting. It looked like the back of someone's head.

"Go over to the sink and wash your hands or something," Stacey suggested. "That way you can really see it."

Maybe whatever Micaela is doing will inspire me, Darci thought. She crossed the art room, glancing at the other students' work as she went. A boy named John was working on an abstract boomerang-shaped thing. A girl named Andy was making a heart-shaped box.

Darci saw the back of Micaela's sculpture first. It was definitely a head, with thick, blunt-cut hair. Something about the back of the head looked familiar, though Darci couldn't quite figure out what it was.

She walked over to the sink, ran some water over her hands, then turned to go back to her chair. That's when she saw the front of Micaela's sculpture.

Darci gasped. She couldn't believe what she was seeing. Everything about the sculpture was perfect—the face, the hair, even the necklace with its delicate heart-shaped pendant resting just below the collarbone. The face had familiar wide-set eyes. And a familiar stubborn chin. The mouth, a touch too wide, was the same mouth that Darci saw every morning in the mirror.

The head that Micaela was capturing so faithfully was hers.

CHAPTER 2

Darci shut her eyes and opened them again. The clay head was still there. She hadn't imagined it.

Fascinated, Darci walked up to the sculpture. It was definitely her—down to the little bump in her nose from the time she'd broken it when she was nine. Stacey was right.

It's so good, it's scary.

"How—how'd you do this?" she stammered.

Micaela ran her thumb along the clay cheekbone, making it more defined. "You're a good model," she said without looking up. "You've got an unusual face."

"I do?"

"Good bones, interesting eyes, strong chin." Micaela spoke with the confidence of someone who was completely sure of her abilities. "Your face has character."

The answer took Darci by surprise. She'd always thought of herself as ordinary-looking. "Maybe," she said, unconvinced. "But I didn't model for you. And I sit way on the other side of the room."

Micaela pointed to the table in front of her. Next to the bust was a page torn from the *Clarion*, the school paper. Darci winced as she saw the familiar headline: NEW STUDENTS IN NORTHRIDGE. The paper had interviewed the kids who'd transferred in this year. Darci thought the article made her sound like an airhead. Even worse was the photograph. Everyone else was flashing white, perfect smiles. Darci, who somehow hadn't heard the photographer say "cheese," was staring morosely into the camera. Kurt said she looked tragically bored.

"Do you like it?" Micaela asked her.

"The photo or the sculpture?" Darci asked wryly.

"Both."

"I hate the picture," Darci confessed. "But your sculpture's different. You make me look—" The word she wanted was *beautiful*. But she was embarrassed to say that aloud. "You make me look better than I do in real life," she said finally.

Micaela nodded. "You look a lot better in person. It's not a great photo."

"Yeah, but you—how did you get so good at sculpture?"

"Working with clay comes easy for me," Micaela replied. "It's probably because I'm a Taurus, an earth sign."

The small stud earrings that Micaela wore gave off a dark green fire in the afternoon light. *Emeralds,* Darci thought. It was occurring to her that Micaela James was a lot more sophisticated than most of the kids she'd met so far at her new school. And she was definitely more sophisticated than anyone at her last school, in New Jersey.

"Are you a senior?" Darci asked.

"Junior," Micaela answered. She gestured toward the article. "You're a sophomore, right? And you're also a water sign. Probably…a Pisces, and probably born in the early part of the sign…a February birthday?"

"February twenty-fourth," Darci said. "How'd you know?"

"Just a guess." Micaela gave a casual shrug. "I've been into astrology for a while now. Each of the elements has certain recognizable characteristics. You've got a soft, dreamy quality that's typical of the water signs. And really small hands and feet. That's very Piscean."

Darci was intrigued. She knew that Pisces, the fish, was her sign. But that was all she knew about the zodiac.

"You're probably a lot better with paint than with clay," Micaela went on.

"I'm really not all that artistic," Darci admitted. "Right now, I can't even figure out how to decorate my room. There's this horrible sludge blue paint on the walls that clashes with my bedspread and everything else I own. It's totally depressing."

Micaela's green eyes lit with interest. "Want some help?" she asked. "We could paint over the blue or find a way to brighten it. You know, maybe use a fabric that will pick up the color."

"That'd be great," Darci said. Her room had bothered her from the day they'd moved in. She just hadn't been able to figure out how to fix it.

"Ladies!" Ms. Yarnell said loudly. "You're supposed to be sculpting, not chattering. Darci, please return to your seat. Micaela, I'm surprised at you. I thought you had better concentration than that."

Micaela flashed Darci a conspirator's grin. "How about today, after school?" she whispered.

"Cool," Darci whispered back. "My locker's right next to the computer lab. Meet you there."

Darci wandered back to her table. Her lump of clay still sat there. It was no more inspiring than it had been before. But Darci's mood had changed completely. For the first time since moving to Northridge, she felt as if she belonged here.

Darci had just made her first new friend.

Darci leaned back in the bucket seat of Micaela's Acura, thoroughly enjoying the ride home. For once, she didn't have to bum a ride off Kurt or endure the endless route of the school bus.

"So how do you like Northridge?" Micaela asked.

"It's okay, so far," Darci answered cautiously.

"You hate it," Micaela translated.

"No," Darci said. "I like this area. The Catskill Mountains are really beautiful—I love the way they're so gentle and rounded. And it's cool living close to the Hudson River. I just thought it would be easier to make friends here. I had a lot of friends back in New Jersey," she added wistfully.

Micaela gave her a bitter smile. "Wait and see. You may not want to make that many friends here."

"What do you mean?"

"Northridge is just so—limited." Micaela nodded at a group of kids gathered on a corner. They were all wearing flannel shirts and baggy jeans. "Everyone here dresses the same, thinks the same, listens to the same music. Sometimes I think that all the kids in that school are clones."

"You should have seen my homeroom on the first day of school," Darci said. "I was the only girl there who *wasn't* wearing Doc Martens."

"The school's a bore," Micaela said dismissively. "Like most high schools. The only cool thing around here is the land. These mountains are really old. I spend a lot of time in the woods, and sometimes I feel like I've wandered into another century. I—"

"Turn left here," Darci broke in as the sign for Weaver's Hill Road appeared. "Sorry. What were you saying?"

"Nothing."

Micaela turned the car onto the winding country road. On either side, trees blazed with autumn color. Darci loved the brilliant golds and reds. There was something exciting about fall in the Catskills—a crispness in the air that seemed to promise clear winter nights blazing with stars and cozy evenings in front of a fire.

"Our house is the last one on the left," Darci said, suddenly feeling self-conscious. She had a feeling that wherever Micaela lived, it was not in a converted summer cottage.

Micaela didn't say anything as she pulled up in

front of the small wood-frame house, except, "Is anyone else home?"

"My mom's away on business this week," Darci explained as they got out of the car. "And my brother Kurt is probably out with the new love of his life: Kristin the Beautiful."

"That's got to be Kris Harper," Micaela said. "What about your dad?"

"He split when I was three," Darci answered in the casual tone she always used when discussing her father. "My mom's never really given us the details. Only that they were too different to live together."

Darci opened the front door. "Ignore the mess," she warned. "It's Box City inside. We've discovered that none of us has a real talent for unpacking." Gingerly, she led the way through the maze of packing cartons that still clogged the living room floor.

In the kitchen, Darci set her books down on the table and peered into the refrigerator. She took out two bottles of sparkling water and gave one to Micaela. "What about you?" she asked. "Any brothers or sisters?"

"A younger brother," Micaela answered. "Devon's four. A little Gemini."

"Devon and Micaela," Darci mused. "Your

parents sure chose unusual names."

"They're unusual people," Micaela said.

"Artists?" Darci guessed.

Micaela laughed. "I wish! They're biochemists. They do research for a pharmaceutical company. My parents live for their experiments. Sometimes I think they can't focus on anything unless it's under a microscope."

"My mom gets distracted, too," Darci said. "She's a sales rep for a publishing company, so she's on the road a lot, always making a zillion calls from her car phone. Kurt and I pretty much take care of each other."

"That's cool," Micaela said. "I mean, after a certain point, parents become unnecessary. Even Devon doesn't really need my parents since they got him a nanny."

Darci looked at Micaela curiously. She *was* different. More sophisticated. More independent. Like no one Darci had ever met before.

The kitchen phone began to ring. "I'd better get that," Darci said. "My mom usually checks in around this time."

"Can I use the bathroom?" Micaela asked.

"It's upstairs," Darci said. "First room on the right. And my room's at the very end of the hall if you want to take a look."

Micaela started up the stairs, and Darci picked up the phone. It wasn't her mother at all. It was Kurt.

"Hey, Darce," he began. "Listen, I'm going to be home a little late tonight…"

Micaela walked up the stairs. But she didn't go to the bathroom. Instead she headed straight for Mrs. Callahan's bedroom, where a phone sat on the bedside night table.

Gently, she lifted the receiver and listened.

"You know it was your turn to cook dinner tonight," she heard Darci say to her brother. "You always find an excuse to get out of it."

"I'll cook for the next two nights," Kurt promised. "Look, Kristin really wants to go to the sale at the Bazaar. I told her I'd take her, and then take her out to dinner."

"I'm thrilled you and Kristin are having such a good time, but…"

"Stop being snotty," Kurt said cheerfully. "I'll see you later tonight. And if you don't want to cook…"

While Kurt started to tell Darci about a frozen lasagna she could heat, Micaela silently replaced the receiver. Moving soundlessly, she made her way down the hallway to the next bedroom. It was definitely Kurt's room. A photograph of Kristin Harper was pinned to the bulletin board.

Kristin, Micaela thought, suppressing a surge of anger. Kristin wasn't part of Micaela's plan. She was going to have to do something about that.

For a moment Micaela stood still, taking in the unmade bed, the pile of clothing on the floor, the stack of CDs next to the CD player. Somehow, she had never imagined that Kurt's room would look like this—as though it might belong to any teenage boy. She fought an urge to look around, to find out as much as she could. But there was no time. Darci would be coming upstairs any minute now. Besides, she'd be in Kurt's room again soon. She was sure of it.

Micaela walked over to the tall pine dresser. On top of it lay the leather choker with the black glass bead that Kurt had worn the first time she saw him. She picked it up and ran her finger along the smooth glass surface, imagining it pressed against his neck. It would do. She slipped it into her pocket.

She gave Kurt's room a last look before moving quietly into the bathroom, where she flushed the toilet and ran water in the sink.

Micaela was in Darci's room when Darci came

upstairs. "I see what you mean about this sludge blue," she said sympathetically.

"Think there's any hope for it?" Darci asked.

"If you're willing to repaint. What's your favorite color?"

"Green," Darci said at once. She knelt on the window seat and stared out at the spruce trees that edged the side of the house. "I really love this view because it looks straight into the treetops. It'd be great if there were a way to get that woodsy feeling into the room."

An interesting problem, Micaela thought. She closed her eyes, picturing several shades of green on the walls. *No*, she decided, *that wouldn't work.*

"If you paint this room green, it will look small and dark," she told Darci. "What about off-white with green trim?"

"I'd have to replace my plaid bedspread..." Darci said doubtfully.

"Why don't we go over to the Bazaar?" Micaela suggested. "They've got great bedspreads, and they're having a sale this week."

"That's really strange," Darci said. "My brother just said that he and Kristin are going to the Bazaar now."

At those words Micaela turned away. "Very strange," she agreed with a smile.

CHAPTER 3

The Bazaar was a huge warehouse filled with imports from every part of the globe. Micaela led the way to the linens section at the back of the store. Darci followed, stopping now and then to picture various items in her room.

She found Micaela sifting through shelves filled with bedspreads and throw pillows.

"See what you think of this." Micaela handed Darci a woven ivory spread. "If you paint your room off-white with a green trim around the windows, you can use this for your spread and maybe add some of these green tapestry pillows…"

Darci saw it at once. "You're right," she said. "That would be perfect. Woodsy and simple and really pretty."

"And"—Micaela picked up a package of ivory lace curtains—"if you want an antique feel, you

could use these. We've got lace curtains in one of
our guest rooms. You should come over sometime—maybe on Saturday—and see if you like
them."

"That'd be great," Darci said. She checked the
price tag on the bedspread. "This is definitely all I
can afford today," she said. "Especially since I have
to buy paint. Maybe I'll come back for the pillows
and curtains later."

"Is that my sister, making plans to buy curtains?" asked a familiar, incredulous voice.

"Hey, Kurt," Darci said. She turned to see her
brother coming toward them, his arm draped
casually around Kristin Harper's shoulders. It was
totally unfair, Darci thought, that Kurt had gotten
all the height genes in the Callahan family. But
even she had to admit that her brother was good-
looking. And he and Kristin made a spectacular
couple.

Kristin was one of those radiantly beautiful
girls. When you looked at her, you couldn't quite
believe she was real. She had big blue eyes with
endless lashes, high cheekbones, and a small,
straight nose. Thick, deep red hair fell to her waist,
setting off her slim form.

Kurt reached out and gave Darci's hair an
affectionate tug. "What are you doing here?"

"Following you, of course," Darci deadpanned. "What do you *think* people do in stores?"

Kurt shot her a mock glare, then smiled when he saw Micaela. Girls, Darci knew, were Kurt's great weakness. He couldn't help himself. He liked them all. He'd had girlfriends since the sixth grade.

Darci figured she'd better make introductions. "Kurt, Kristin, this is Micaela James."

"Micaela and I already know each other from school," Kristin said in a cool voice.

"Nice to meet you," Kurt said, extending his hand to Micaela. "Are you part of the curtains expedition here?"

"Micaela's been giving me great ideas for redecorating my room," Darci explained.

Micaela shrugged modestly. "I like working with color," she said. She studied Kurt for a moment. "You and Darci don't look anything alike."

"Darce takes after our mom's side of the family," Kurt explained. "I take after our dad's."

"You're what—a Leo?" Micaela asked.

Kurt's gray eyes widened in surprise. His expression became skeptical as he saw Darci smiling. "You told her, didn't you?"

"I didn't say a word!" Darci protested indignantly.

"She didn't," Micaela assured him. "I just guessed. It's sort of a game I like to play—to see if I can guess people's signs. And, Kristin, you've got to be a Scorpio."

"Right again," Kristin said, her voice even chillier.

"So what are you guys shopping for?" Darci asked, trying to keep the conversation light.

Kristin didn't answer. Instead she glanced at her watch, then looped her arm through Kurt's. "We'd better go," she told him. "I don't want to be late for our dinner reservation."

Darci couldn't believe this. Since when did Kurt go to the kind of restaurant where you needed a reservation?

Kurt nodded at his sister. "You have a ride home?"

"I'll drive Darci home," Micaela offered.

"Cool," Kurt said. "Later, Darce."

"Later," Darci echoed. "Bye, Kristin."

Kristin acted as if she hadn't even heard her. Darci watched as Kurt and Kristin left the store, their arms wrapped around each other.

"Is it me or is she always so rude?" Darci asked Micaela.

Micaela smiled. "It's not you. Scorpions can't help stinging. Don't pay any attention to her."

Darci sighed. Somehow, meeting up with Kristin always left her feeling hurt and awkward.

"Come on," Micaela said gently. "Let's pay for that bedspread. Then we can get a pizza."

"I can't," Darci said. "The bedspread is my allowance for the last two weeks. All of it."

"The pizza's my treat," Micaela assured her. "I've got a rich grandmother who spoils me rotten."

"Do you really?"

"How do you think I got my own car?" Micaela asked as they walked toward the front of the store. "Grandma was a sculptor when she was young. She still doesn't understand how her own daughter wound up a scientist. She identifies with me because I'm artistic. She says I'm the only one in the family she can talk to. So she's always been very generous with me."

"You're awfully lucky," Darci said.

"Yes, I am," Micaela replied quietly.

Darci took her place on the end of a long line at the register. Micaela stood behind her, looking at the jewelry displayed inside the glass counter.

"Could I see that?" Micaela asked the salesgirl. She pointed to an elaborate silver ring set with turquoise and coral.

The girl took the ring out of the case and

handed it to Micaela. Micaela slid it easily onto her ring finger. "What do you think?" she asked Darci.

"Nice," Darci said. "Where's it from?"

"India," Micaela replied. "Watch." She touched the side of the ring and its top flipped open. The top, Darci saw, was hollowed out inside.

"It's like a locket," Darci said.

Micaela and the salesgirl exchanged an unreadable look. "Not exactly," Micaela said. "This is supposed to be the kind of ring the Borgias used to wear. It was used for something very different."

"The Borgias," Darci said. "We studied them last year in world history. They were a ruling family in medieval France, right?"

"Renaissance Italy," Micaela corrected her. "Do you remember what they were famous for?"

"They were…really powerful and ruthless."

"Exactly."

"So what's that got to do with a ring?"

"One of the things the Borgias were famous for was the way they disposed of their enemies," Micaela said. "The legend is, they had their jewelers make them rings like this for a very specific purpose." She closed the ring with a snap. "They called them poison rings."

CHAPTER 4

Kurt had nearly finished his dinner when he realized that Kristin was being unusually quiet.

"Is your food okay?" he asked her.

She nodded, poking at her shrimp scampi.

"Well, then how about everything else? You've hardly said a word since we left the Bazaar."

"I've been thinking," Kristin said, but she didn't elaborate. Kurt wondered if her silence had anything to do with meeting Micaela James. Micaela was definitely intriguing—and Kristin definitely didn't like her.

He studied Kristin's face. In the candlelight her eyes seemed a darker shade of blue, and her hair shone red-gold. Kurt had always had girlfriends. Nearly all of them had been pretty. But Kristin was more than pretty. Kristin was the most beautiful creature he'd ever seen. Part of him was conceited enough to think he had a real chance when he asked her out. And the rest of him still couldn't believe she'd said yes.

"Penny for your thoughts?" he said.

"They're worth more than that," Kristin told him, her voice teasing.

"Okay, so just what are your thoughts worth?"

"Oh…"—Kristin's eyes studied the ceiling—"maybe tickets to the Luka Bloom concert next week."

"Done," Kurt said easily. "But you could have just asked me."

Kristin shook her head. "Not my style."

It's true, he thought. Kristin was rarely straightforward about what she wanted. She preferred to manipulate people. He didn't think it was evil or even deliberate. It was just the way that Kristin Harper operated.

"Okay," Kurt said. "But since I agreed to the concert, you've got to tell me—how come you haven't said a word through this entire meal?"

"I was just wondering," Kristin said. "Is your little sister always going to be tagging along with us?"

That was the last thing Kurt had been expecting. "What do you mean?"

"Well, she followed you tonight."

"Darci was just busting me when she said that," Kurt explained. "She and Micaela went to the Bazaar to find things for her room."

"It just seems as if Darci's very dependent on you," Kristin said in a reasonable tone.

Kurt ran a hand through his sandy hair, trying to find a way to explain things. Kristin was an only child, he knew. She wasn't used to brothers or sisters. And she lived in the same town she'd been born in. She hadn't just moved. She had tons of friends.

"Darci's just a little shy, that's all," he said at last. "We're new in town, and she hasn't made many friends yet. Besides, she and I get along."

Kristin finished the last of her iced tea. "I just think Darci needs to stand on her own feet a little more."

"She will," Kurt said. "Give her some time."

"I know." Kristin's voice softened. "I'm sure things will change. After all, now she's got someone she can hang out with. That girl—Micaela…"

That night, after Micaela dropped Darci at her house she drove east, into the Catskill Mountains. The road was dark. A narrow, winding road with forest on either side. There were no houses or stores or even gas stations out here. During the day, hikers and backpackers frequented the trails in the area. By night the road was deserted.

Micaela pulled over onto a narrow shoulder and parked the car behind a thick growth of brush. A short distance from the car were two stone gateposts with a heavy chain connecting them and a sign warning off trespassers. Micaela knew that parts of the Catskill preserve were privately owned. She'd heard rumors that whoever owned this section lived in a fortress-like compound on top of the ridge. But she'd never seen anyone down here. And she'd been coming here for years. First by day, but now she always came at night.

She shut off the car lights, got out, and took seven empty gallon containers and a small backpack from the trunk. She put three of the jugs into the pack and carried the others by hand. Then she slipped beneath the chain and onto the wooded mountain path.

The sky was lit by a thin crescent moon, enough light for her to find her way. Micaela had always had keen night vision, and these woods were as familiar to her as her own yard. The sounds of the owls didn't startle her. She was used to the raccoons and foxes, to the deer who moved through the trees as quietly as ghosts. Even in the dark, she could identify the different kinds of trees. She knew these woods like she knew herself.

She continued uphill on a narrow footpath, welcoming the ache in her calves, the cool night air against her face, the sweet scent of earth and forest. Here and in her garden were the places she felt most alive.

The ground leveled off, and she continued along another path until she reached the spring. Years ago, someone else had found it. Someone had put in a small copper pipe with a spigot that was now green with age.

One by one, Micaela began to fill the containers with water from the spring. This would feed her garden. Pure, clear, ice-cold water straight from the heart of the mountain. Her parents, she knew, would probably not believe her theory: that this water collected from this place, always beneath the moon, was the lifeblood of her garden. It was the reason every plant was so strong, so healthy, so perfect. Her parents would say that wasn't scientific. Then again, her parents had never seen her garden. And they never would.

Micaela filled and sealed the last of the seven containers. She returned three to the pack and put the pack on her shoulders. The other four jugs she carried in her hands. She made her way back down the mountain to her car, used to the weight of the water.

She loaded the containers into the trunk and set off for home. For the first time since she'd dropped off Darci, she let her thoughts return to the Callahan family. Darci and her good-looking brother. Micaela remembered the way he'd looked at Kristin in the Bazaar. Something inside Kurt lit up every time he looked at the beautiful red-haired girl.

It's strange, Micaela thought. She couldn't believe she was actually jealous of that airhead Kris Harper. Kristin had something she wanted. Something Micaela was meant to have.

The voice has never been wrong, Micaela told herself. Kris might not be part of the plan, but she wasn't a serious obstacle either. It was only a matter of time before Kurt fell for her and gave up Kristin. And if he didn't…Micaela's thoughts returned to her garden. She was sure there was something in the garden that would take care of Kris Harper.

Micaela waited until dark. Once again, luck was with her. Not only was there no moon, but thick clouds filled the skies, concealing even the tiniest glimmer of starlight.

She waited until everyone was fast asleep. Until the midnight hour had come. And then, soundlessly, she slipped out of the house and into the garden.

Rain had fallen all that week. The scent of damp earth rose from the ground, and a sharp wind moved through the trees.

She shivered in the cold night air. Beneath her thick wool cloak, her skin was bare. She grasped the handle of a woven basket in one hand, a heavy glass pitcher in the other. Her bare feet ached with cold as she made her way across the frost-covered ground. She moved swiftly past the thorn-covered rose bushes and the hydrangea beds, past the azaleas and lilies, to the very back of the property, where a tall stone wall bordered the yard.

The wall was older than the house, built late in the eighteenth century. Its flat, broad stones had been laid by hand, fitted together so tightly and neatly that no mortar was ever needed. Now the wall lay hidden beneath a thick tangle of vines.

She set down the basket and the pitcher and reached into the vines. The icy leaves numbed her hands, but she paid no attention to her own discomfort. As she'd done so many times before, she removed nine stones from the edge of the wall. She worked carefully, patiently, so that they could be set back in place. So that no one would ever know they'd been touched.

With the stones piled neatly at her feet, there was only a thick curtain of vines between her and what lay on the other side of the wall. Gently, she parted the vines and slid the basket and the pitcher through to the other side. Still shaking from the cold, she climbed through.

She felt her body relax as soon she stepped through to the other side of the wall. She was in a small, rectangular garden, enclosed by four stone walls. When she'd first found it, it had been overgrown with weeds. She'd never found out who created the hidden garden or why. Only one thing was certain: No one else knew about it. And so it had become hers.

Three springs past, she'd planted the first bulbs. Death camas. In the summer they'd bloomed with clusters of green-white starlike flowers. Tonight they were no more than slender green stalks planted in a circle. Now she watched them dance in the cold night wind. They seemed to be alive.

She drew in her breath sharply as she dropped her cloak and stepped into the center of the circle. Though the cold bit at her skin, she forced herself to remain still. Not to resist the elements but to be part of them. This was the one place in the world that was hers and hers alone. This was where she was strong and powerful and beautiful. This was where she worked the earth's magic.

She called on the elements: fire, water, air, and earth. She called on the energies of the four directions. She called on the nine planets and the sun, moon, and stars. She called on wind and thunder, lightning and rain. Finally she called on the powers of darkness.

And when she felt them all moving inside her, she stepped out of the circle. She stood for a moment, noting what was already in place. She'd planted the edges of the garden three springs past. White and red baneberry bushes against the northern wall. Pink sheep laurel mixed with white water hemlock against the southern. Her favorite, purple foxglove, ran along the western edge of the garden, and the shiny black berries of deadly nightshade bordered the east. Some of the seeds she'd ordered from special catalogs. Others she'd gathered and dried herself. She'd put them in earth, fed them water and nutrients, and kept them under a grow light in her room until they were ready to be part of the garden.

Wrapping herself in the cloak, she bent down and reached into the basket. She was glad she hadn't waited any longer. The first frost of the winter would set in soon. She took out clippers and carefully began to harvest her crop. First she cut from the white hellebore, then the delicate blue-violet lobelia and the dark purple monkshood. Finally, she took cuttings from the newest addition to the garden. Something she'd only just discovered. The plant was related to the foxglove, its flowers even more beautiful. Dark reddish flowers shaped like hearts. The plant didn't even have a popular name yet. Just something unpronounceable in Latin. She thought of it as Hearts of Darkness. She ran a fingertip across the stems. They were so delicate, it was hard to believe they'd survive this cold night. But she knew they would.

"Hearts of Darkness for the dark," she whispered as she set them in the basket.

When she'd taken her cuttings, she watered the plants she'd cut with the spring water in the glass pitcher.

Her work done, she surveyed the garden with satisfaction. Every plant within the walls was beautiful. Most were fragrant. And each and every one of them was poison.

CHAPTER 5

Lunchtime was Darci's least favorite time of day. And Fridays were the worst. Everyone was talking about all the things they'd do together on the weekend. Everyone but Darci. She stood at the edge of the cafeteria, wondering where to sit.

Not by the windows—that area belonged to the jocks. And not in front, where all the nerds talked computerese at each other. And certainly not at the table she'd tried yesterday. Darci had wanted to die when Monica Williams turned to her and said, "Don't you have someplace else you can sit?"

She'd just about decided to brave one of the nerd tables when a voice behind her said, "What do you say we blow off the cafeteria?"

Darci turned to see a boy she recognized from her elective European history class. Although he was a junior, Ian Hassler was only about two inches taller than Darci. He had thick, straight collar-length black hair and very tanned skin. His eyes were a light hazel brown, and there was something about his expression that made her think he found the whole world very amusing.

"Can we leave the school?" Darci asked.

Ian shrugged. "We *can* do anything we want. We're not *supposed* to, if that's what you're asking. If we get caught, we'll probably get detentions."

Darci took another look at the crowded cafeteria, reeking of steam-table food, and made an instant decision. "Let's go," she said.

Ian nodded and led the way through the halls to the very back of the school. He opened the door to the parking lot, then made his way over the low brick wall to a sloping, grass-covered hillside. He settled down beneath an oak tree and took a brown paper bag from his pack.

Darci sat next to him, feeling a little self-conscious. She didn't know Ian at all, and here she was, sitting beside him.

Ian didn't seem bothered by the situation. He took a sandwich out of a paper bag. "Do you have lunch?"

"No," Darci admitted, feeling a little foolish. "I was going to buy."

"Let me spare you." Ian handed her half a sandwich. "A very delicate and exotic gourmet treat, known locally as peanut butter and jelly," he explained. "And"—he reached into the paper bag and pulled out a bag of barbecued chips—"spiced slices of fried potato."

Darci giggled. "I can't eat your lunch!"

"Sure you can. Bring me half a sandwich and half a bag of chips tomorrow, and we'll be even."

"Okay," Darci agreed. This impromptu picnic in the warm October sun was totally doing it for her.

"So," Ian said, "you finding it hard to be the new kid in Clique City?"

"How'd you know?"

"I did it last year," he confessed. "Let's just say it's not an experience I'd want to repeat."

"But you have friends now," Darci said. "Whenever I see you, you're surrounded by other kids."

Ian raised one dark eyebrow. "So you've been watching me?"

"I didn't say that!" Darci protested, feeling herself blush.

Ian bit back a grin. "Well, I've been watching you."

"Why?"

Ian shrugged. "I don't know," he admitted. "I guess I can't help it. I like you."

"You don't know me," Darci pointed out.

"But I'd like to," Ian said.

Darci studied his face, wondering if he was being straight with her. Ever since the first day of school, she *had* been watching Ian. He was definitely one of the more outstanding guys in school. In fact, she'd already decided that he was too good-looking and popular to be attracted to her.

Ian's brown eyes met her own, warm and direct. "I watch you in history class," he said. "I like the way you always try to put things together—you make connections, find patterns in the past. You're interesting." He took a deep breath, as if gathering his courage, then added, "And you also happen to be cute."

Darci didn't know how to respond to that. No boy had ever said anything like that to her before, and she wasn't quite bold enough to say she thought he was cute, too. "How come your family moved to Northridge?" she asked instead.

"Good question," he said in a quiet, bitter voice.

"You don't know?"

"I know, all right. I'm just not wild about the answer."

"Forget I asked," Darci said quickly. She finished her half of the sandwich and then said, "We moved here because my mom's job transferred her."

"Your dad didn't mind?" Ian asked.

"He wasn't around to object. He cut out a long time ago."

"My dad kind of cut out, too." Ian stared straight ahead of him. "The reason we left Albany," he said in a slow, deliberate voice, "is because my father embezzled money. He's in prison now."

"I'm sorry," Darci said at once.

"I'm not." Ian's voice went cold with anger. "My father's been lying to people since the day he was born. He was always betraying someone, always selling someone out. We all knew he was going to get caught. It's a relief to finally have it over with."

"Are you really glad he's in jail?" Darci asked.

Ian turned to her and the anger went out of his eyes. "No," he admitted. "I hate to think of him in there, but I'm glad he can't hurt anyone else for a while. He—he did a lot of damage."

Gently, Ian reached out and took Darci's hand in his own. "I'm sorry," he said. "I didn't mean to dump the family soap opera on you. I usually don't talk about it at all."

"That's okay," Darci said. "Every family's got its own built-in soap opera."

"Yeah, well, ours is a disaster," Ian assured her. "But on a lighter note, I'm going skating with a bunch of kids on Saturday. Wanna come?"

"Sure," Darci began. Then she caught herself. "I mean, no, I can't."

"Why not?" Ian asked, sounding a little hurt.

"Because someone else—Micaela James— invited me over to her house on Saturday," Darci explained.

"Micaela…she's a junior, right? Long blond hair, seriously artistic?"

"She's in my art class," Darci said. "And she's helping me redo my room."

Ian was silent for a moment, then stood up. "How well do you know Micaela?" he asked.

"About as well as I know you," Darci answered. "I talked to her for the first time this week. Why?"

"She's got a weird rep," Ian said bluntly.

Darci stood up to face him. "What do you mean? That she doesn't act like everyone else in this school? I thought you were the one who didn't like Clique City."

Ian raked his heel in the dirt. "This isn't about cliques," he said at last. "I don't know Micaela very well, but I've heard she's into some pretty strange stuff."

"Like what?"

"Like hanging out in the cemetery on Halloween. The rumor is, she was trying to raise the dead."

"You don't really believe that?" Darci asked, incredulous.

"I don't know what to believe," Ian said. "I know that most kids steer clear of her, and I think there's probably a good reason for that."

Darci didn't for a minute believe the crazy rumors about Micaela, yet Ian's belief that there was something wrong with her was unsettling.

"What if I want to be her friend?" Darci asked. "Does that mean you and I can't be friends?"

Ian's tawny eyes met Darci's. "No," he said. "Micaela James has nothing to do with you and me."

"Then how about we go skating another time?" Darci suggested.

Ian gave her a crooked smile. "You got it," he said. "Just remember, you owe me half a sandwich and half a bag of chips." He glanced at his watch. "Come on, lunch period's almost over. We'd better go back inside before someone notices we're gone."

*   *   *

Micaela walked up to Darci as she stood at her locker, getting her books for the afternoon. She wore a black tunic-length sweater over tight black jeans with black lace-up boots. Her hair hung loose, a mass of silver-blond waves.

"Where were you?" Micaela asked Darci. "I saw you come back in from outside."

Darci debated a moment before answering, then decided that having lunch with Ian shouldn't be a secret from her friend. "I ate outside," she answered. "I had lunch with Ian Hassler."

"Ian Hassler," Micaela repeated slowly. "He transferred in last year from Albany. I heard there was some scandal about his father. He got popped for murder or something."

"There's no scandal and definitely no murder," Darci said, wanting to set the record straight. "Ian's very upfront about it. His dad was caught embezzling money, and he's doing time for it now. It's over."

Micaela leaned against Darci's locker. "Ian's an Aries, you know. He wouldn't be any good for you. He's much too pushy and self-centered."

Darci shook her head in amazement. "All we did was eat a sandwich together," she said. "You're making it sound like we're ready to get married."

Micaela smiled. "Don't worry," she said. "You

won't. I guarantee it."

Micaela sat at her desk, concentrating on the mound of reddish powder on the marble cutting board in front of her. It was late Saturday morning. Her parents had given Devon's nanny the day off and taken him to the zoo. It was one of those rare times when she had the house to herself—which was the only reason she could do this. She could finally see just what it was the Hearts of Darkness would yield.

She reached out, touched the reddish powder with her fingertip, and touched just a bit of it to her tongue. It was completely tasteless, as it should be. Then she sniffed at it—it was odorless, too. The problem was the color. She dropped a bit in a glass of water, and frowned as the water took on a reddish tinge. She'd have to do something about that. The powder had to be tasteless, odorless, and colorless. She made some notes in the open notebook to the side of the cutting board.

The other questions, of course, had to do with strength. How much of the powder would she need to affect someone? And how long would it take before it kicked in? She'd already tried a minuscule dose on a mouse. Ten minutes after ingesting the powder, the mouse went into convulsions and died. She was surprised it had taken so long.

What she needed, she realized, was a test. She needed to try a small dose on a human guinea pig. Not a dangerous dose, just enough to gauge what she'd need for the full effect.

On the desk, just behind the cutting board, was a milligram scale that Micaela had taken from her parents' lab. Carefully, she measured out a small dose of the reddish powder.

A sound from the front of the house caught her attention. Micaela turned and peered out her window. A Toyota pulled into the circular drive. Darci sat in the passenger seat. Beside her sat a dark-haired woman who was probably her mother.

Quickly, Micaela started to clear her desk. She poured the reddish powder into a small glass vial—except for the powder in the scale, which she carefully scooped into her poison ring. The cutting board, scale, and the mortar and pestle that she used to grind the dried flowers she tucked away in the bottom of the huge wooden wardrobe that held her clothing. The notebook she slid into a desk drawer.

Micaela surveyed her room, wondering what Darci would make of this place. Of the candles and the tapestries, of the four-poster bed and the crystal ball on the fireplace mantel, of the Chinese doctor's chest with its dozens of tiny wooden drawers, of the bookshelf filled with books on astrology, the tarot, crystalomancy, and magic.

She lit candles and put a disk of medieval music on the CD player. Almost everything was ready. All she needed was something to offer Darci—sparkling water mixed with cranberry juice, she decided. Red…the right color for hiding Hearts of Darkness.

She went downstairs to the kitchen, where she chose two large glasses, one a deep blue and the other a deep green. As she filled them with the juice mixture, Micaela thought about Darci. She was the perfect way to get to Kurt. And she'd make a perfect friend. She was young and unsophisticated for a sophomore. Smart but unsure of herself. Very impressionable. And lonely. She'd been in Northridge for over a month now, and she still didn't fit in. Ian Hassler seemed interested in her, but that wouldn't last long. Micaela knew exactly how to take care of Ian.

Micaela tapped the contents of her ring into the blue glass. She wanted Darci exactly the way she'd been on the day she first saw her at the diner—just dying for someone to be her friend.

CHAPTER 6

"This is where your friend lives?" Mrs. Callahan asked, her voice rising with surprise.

"I guess so," Darci said, trying to sound casual. Her mother had driven down a long private road that led to a circular drive in front of a huge three-story stone house. Maybe *house* was the wrong word. *Mansion* came closer.

"One seventy-five Blackburn Lane," Darci read from the paper where she'd scrawled Micaela's address. "Yup, this is it. That's Micaela's Acura parked on the side there."

"Well, have a good time," her mother said. "And call if you need a ride home."

"Uh-huh," Darci said, getting out of the car. She barely noticed her mother pulling away. She was awed by the Jameses' house. Feeling a little nervous, Darci approached the door and rang the bell.

Seconds later Micaela came to the door, wearing faded jeans and an oversize man's white shirt. Darci was relieved to see her dressed so casually. She'd almost expected Micaela to answer the door dressed in a formal gown.

"Come on in," Micaela said. "My parents are out with Devon, so we've got the place to ourselves."

Darci followed Micaela through a high-ceilinged entryway to a wooden stairway. Peering over the carved banister, she could see a spacious living room with floor-to-ceiling windows.

"The living room opens onto the gardens," Micaela said. "I'll give you the full tour later, if you like."

"Definitely," Darci said. She felt as if she'd stepped into a decorator's magazine. Oriental carpets covered the stone floors. The furniture was old and made from heavy dark wood. Darci smiled as she realized that the oak chair in front of the hearth was carved in the shape of two griffins: their heads formed the armrests, their wings swept around to form the back of the chair.

"This place is amazing," Darci said.

"It's been in the family since 1850," Micaela told her. "Both my grandmother and my mother were born here. Grandma lived here until I was eight. She's also a Taurus and a total antique fiend—she bought furniture the way other people buy groceries. Then she developed asthma and decided to retire to Palm Springs. So she bought a house there and gave this place to us."

"Some gift."

"Taureans are very materialistic," Micaela admitted. "We like being surrounded by nice things."

At the end of a hallway on the third floor, Micaela opened a wooden door with a trumpet-shaped flower carved on it. Darci followed her into the room, feeling as if she'd walked into a dream. The walls were a pale yellow, the Oriental carpet that covered the floor all deep blues and reds. A flowered tapestry spread covered the four-poster bed. Another tapestry depicting a medieval hunt hung from the wall. White calla lilies stood in a blue glass vase on top of Micaela's dresser, and a crystal ball topped the fireplace mantel. Flowering plants covered a brass table in one corner of the room and crowded the windowsills. A delicate mix of flower perfumes filled the air. Everything in the room seemed rich and fine and incredibly exotic.

Darci didn't know where to look first. Everything in Micaela's room was exquisite. But her eyes kept being drawn back to the plants. Purple, red, and blue flowers cascaded over the windowsill and made the brass table a kaleidoscope of lush color. "You have an incredible green thumb," she said at last. "I've never seen so many gorgeous plants in one place."

"Can't help it," Micaela said. "I'm a Taurus, the first of the earth signs. If I don't grow things, I start to get out of touch with myself."

Darci curled up in an armchair that was covered in wine red velvet. She glanced at a reproduction of one of van Gogh's sunflowers that hung on Micaela's wall. "Not like old Vincent," she said. "He was so intense he cut off his ear. That's a little too intense for me."

"The intensity is what allowed him to be a great artist," Micaela said fiercely. "Every artist has to be intense, and driven, so they can overcome incredible obstacles. But something happened to van Gogh at the end. No one really knows whether he was sick or insane or what."

Darci reflected that most of the conversations with her friends in N.J. had been about boys or clothes. Now here she was, in this incredible room, talking art with Micaela. "How do you know all this stuff?" Darci asked.

"I'm driven, too," Micaela said with a smile. "For a long time now, I've known that I'm going to be an artist. So I read up on other artists. There's something about van Gogh that intrigues me."

Darci was beginning to think that Micaela James was the most extraordinary person she'd ever met. What she couldn't quite figure out was why Micaela had chosen her for a friend.

"I want to show you something," Micaela said. She got up, pulled a thick paperback from the bookshelf and handed it to Darci.

Darci thumbed through the pages and saw that the book was filled with columns of numbers. "What is this?" she asked.

"It's called an ephemeris. It shows where everything in the solar system is at any given moment. If you know your birthplace and birth time, you can use the ephemeris to figure out where each of the planets was when you were born," Micaela explained.

"Oh," Darci said.

Micaela opened one of her desk drawers and pulled out a chart. It showed a circle divided into twelve sections. Each section was inked in with astrological signs. "This is my birth chart," Micaela said. "See, you can use the ephemeris to draw up a chart and plot your horoscope. Why don't you have a look? I'll go downstairs and get us something to drink."

Darci paged through the ephemeris, but she couldn't really make much sense of it. And trying to read Micaela's birth chart was like trying to decipher hieroglyphics.

A few minutes later, Micaela returned, holding two glasses. She handed Darci the blue one. "Cranberry juice and sparkling water," she said. "That okay?"

"Fine." Darci took a sip and handed the chart back to Micaela. "I really don't know how to read this," she admitted. "It's sort of overwhelming."

Micaela began to point to the sections of the chart. "I was born on May tenth, which means my birth sign or sun sign is Taurus. I've got Scorpio rising, and the moon and Uranus conjunct the ascendant with a hard aspect to Neptune."

Darci winced. "Could you translate that into English, please? It's like you're talking a different language."

Micaela settled back on the bed. "Sorry," she said. "Those terms are just a way of talking about the influences of different planets. The way the moon, Uranus, and Neptune work on each other in my chart means that I've got strong artistic influences and strong—but unpredictable— psychic influences."

"Sounds very mysterious and romantic," Darci said a little enviously. "What does Scorpio do?"

"Nothing as mysterious or romantic," Micaela assured her. "For me, Taurus and Scorpio add up to perseverance. They're both fixed signs. They never give up on anything."

Darci took another sip of the drink. "Can you tell what my influences are?" she asked curiously.

"To do a proper horoscope, we'd have to draw up a chart for you," Micaela said. "Most charts are done by computer, but I can probably figure out the basics of yours. I'll need the date, place, and exact time of your birth."

Darci gave Micaela the information, then watched as Micaela made some calculations, and began to page through the ephemeris, taking notes.

"Let's see…Pisces is your sun sign. That means Pisces is your essence or inner self, the true you. And Taurus is your rising sign. That explains it."

Darci finished the cranberry soda. "Explains what?"

"Why you and I get along," Micaela said. "I've got Taurus as my sun sign and you've got it as your rising sign. We each respect and like the Taurus in the other."

Darci was still a little puzzled. "What exactly is a rising sign?" she asked.

"Your rising sign—or ascendant—is the constellation that was rising on the eastern horizon at the hour that you were born," Micaela answered. "The characteristics of the rising sign form your outer personality—the you that you show to the rest of the world. It's also a kind of progression—the traits you'll grow into in this lifetime."

"You mean I'm going to become materialistic?" Darci asked.

"Materialistic and stubborn," Micaela assured her. "And you're probably going to develop quite a temper."

Darci laughed at the prediction. "That's something to look forward to."

Micaela continued to take notes from the ephemeris. "I've got to put the whole chart together to give you an accurate reading," she said. "But so far, your stars look good. Your sun sign, Pisces, is water; and your rising sign, Taurus, is earth. Those two are very complementary—that means you'll have an easy time overcoming obstacles and achieving your goals."

Darci rolled her eyes. "Kurt says I always try to get out of having to deal."

"That's because it's easy for the fish to swim around barriers," Micaela said. "I bet your brother has a different approach. The lion usually enjoys a good fight."

"Kurt isn't afraid of conflict, that's for sure," Darci agreed. She stood up and went to stand by one of the windows. She felt a little strange. Her heart was beating faster and she was mildly nauseated—as if she was about to get sick but wasn't quite there yet. Idly, she trailed one hand through the plants on the sill.

"Don't!" Micaela said sharply. "Their leaves are very delicate and you might bruise them."

"Sorry," Darci said. She shut her eyes, hoping the weird feeling would go away. She loved being here at Micaela's; the last thing she wanted was to get sick now. Trying to distract herself, she turned the conversation back to astrology. "You really believe in the zodiac?"

"You make it sound like a religion," Micaela said. "It's not like that. The point of the zodiac is fate. That certain paths are ordained for all of us. Your horoscope is simply a map of the paths that are open to you."

Darci fought another wave of nausea and nodded toward Micaela's chart. "So what kind of paths does fate have in store for you?"

"My stars are very strong," Micaela answered. She glanced around her room with a rueful smile. "A lot of things come easily to me."

"And if they don't?" Darci asked.

"I told you," Micaela said quietly. "I'm very driven. I don't let anything get in my way."

Darci clasped her hand over her mouth as the nausea intensified.

"I-I need to use your bathroom—" she mumbled.

"This way," Micaela said, looking alarmed. Quickly she led Darci down the hall to a bathroom.

Mortified, Darci shut the door, leaned over the toilet and heaved. But nothing came up. After a few minutes the nausea passed, and she rinsed her face and went back into Micaela's room.

"Are you okay?" Micaela asked, clearly worried.

Darci nodded. "I think so. I-I—" Her arms and legs started to shake. She fell to the floor, unable to stand. Her muscles were contracting, spasmodic. Her body was twisting wildly, totally out of control.

Micaela's green eyes widened. "Oh, my God, Darci," she said, "I think you're having convulsions. Don't die, Darce—it isn't time!"

CHAPTER 7

Micaela stood over her bed, watching Darci's sleeping form. The Hearts of Darkness worked even better than she'd expected. She was glad she'd given Darci such a small amount. Any more and there would have been serious damage.

Darci looked so young and trusting when she slept. Micaela almost felt protective of her. Almost. She leaned forward and, with a delicate pair of gold scissors, snipped a lock of Darci's hair from the back of her head.

Working carefully, Micaela bound the hair with black thread and placed it in a midnight blue silk pouch. Crossing the room, she slipped the pouch into one of the narrow wooden drawers in the Chinese doctor's chest, next to the drawer that contained hemlock and hellebore seeds.

Minutes later, Darci's eyes fluttered open. She blinked and then opened them wide. "Micaela?" she asked in an unsteady voice.

"Right here," Micaela said.

"What—what just happened?" Darci asked.

Micaela shrugged. "You said you weren't feeling well and went to the bathroom. Then you came back in here and told me you were tired and asked if you could rest for a while. You fell asleep on my bed. You probably have a touch of the flu. There's a lot of weird stuff going around Northridge lately."

Darci sat up and rubbed her forehead. "No, it was more than that," she said. "I was convulsing. Right there on your floor. I was so scared. You ordered me not to die…it wasn't time. And then I think I lost consciousness."

"Darce." Micaela sat down on the bed beside her. "You must have dreamed that part."

"No," Darci said. "It was too vivid. When I was dreaming, I dreamed about Ian. But the convulsions—"

"Believe me," Micaela cut in. "If you were really sick, I would have called 911. You just fell asleep."

Darci shut her eyes. "It seemed so real."

Micaela put her hand to Darci's forehead. "You might be a little feverish," she said. "Do you want me to take you home?"

"No," Darci said. "I think I'm okay now."

Micaela smiled. "You're fine," she said. "Trust me, everything's going to be just fine."

On Monday, Ian stood at his locker, debating whether or not to cut fourth-period geometry. The idea was tempting. Geometry bored the living daylights out of him. But he'd cut last week and nearly got caught. Besides, he reasoned, if he went to geometry, he'd pass Darci in the hall on her way to Spanish. And right now, he was willing to put up with geometry if it meant seeing Darci.

"Hey, dude!" John Leone pounded him on the shoulder. "You coming to soccer practice today?"

Ian slammed his locker shut and started down the hall alongside him. "I'm thinking about it."

"That's really good of you," John said, "considering that we have a game tomorrow, and Southridge almost beat us last time. Tomorrow they beg."

Ian let that pass without comment. He liked playing soccer and he was good at it. Last year he'd been the only sophomore chosen for the varsity team. Still, he couldn't help thinking all the school competitive stuff was dumb. It was hard for him to get too psyched about whether Northridge won or lost the conference title.

The two boys turned the corner of the hallway. Darci should be coming out of chemistry class about now, Ian figured. Just knowing he would see her soon made school more bearable. Darci wasn't a knockout like Kristin Harper, but when he talked to her he felt as though they'd been friends forever. There was something about Darci Callahan that Ian liked and trusted.

"Would you do me a favor and get lost for a few minutes?" he said to John.

"Why?"

"Just do it," Ian said. "I'll explain later."

Looking mildly offended, John stopped at a water fountain and began horsing around with another guy from the soccer team.

Suddenly Ian saw Darci coming out of the chemistry lab. She looked crestfallen. "What happened to you?" he asked with concern.

"I just nearly blew up the school," Darci confessed.

"Not a bad idea," Ian joked.

"I was feeling really weird on Saturday. Then yesterday I thought I was okay, but today I spaced and put the wrong white powder in the beaker,"

Darci went on miserably. "I don't even know what it was. All I know is, all of a sudden Mr. Finn was running down the aisle, waving a fire extinguisher at me."

"Did he use it?" Ian asked, his eyes dancing with amusement.

"No," Darci said. "The fire burned itself out pretty quickly. But I don't think that helped my grade any. This is _such_ a Monday, I can't believe it!"

The first bell for fourth period rang then. "I'd better go," Darci said, sounding worried. "I was late for Spanish on Friday, and Señora Diaz nearly had a cow—excuse me, a _vaca_."

Ian laughed. "How about we do something this week? Maybe a movie?"

Darci glanced at her watch. "I'll talk to you about it later," she promised, and hurried off.

Ian sighed and headed toward geometry. Well, they sort of had a date. Maybe next time he saw Darci, he'd do something really courageous, like ask for her phone number.

"You're Ian Hassler, aren't you?" said a voice behind him.

Ian turned to see a tall blond girl in a tight brown velvet dress walking toward him. Smoky quartz set in silver hung from her ears, and the dress's low-cut neckline revealed a matching necklace. There was no mistaking Micaela James. Ian didn't particularly like her, but, like most of the guys in school, he couldn't help appreciating her looks.

The second bell for fourth period rang. Ian ignored it, wondering why Micaela suddenly wanted to talk to him.

"I saw you with Darci Callahan," Micaela began. "So I thought it was only fair to warn you."

"Warn me of what?" Ian asked.

"Darci's sweet," Micaela said. "But she can't keep her mouth shut."

The halls were empty now. Everyone was in class except for Ian and Micaela.

"What are you talking about?" Ian asked.

Micaela shrugged. "Well, it's just that this morning Darci told me and a bunch of other kids that your dad's upstate, doing time for embezzlement."

"Wh-what?" Ian stammered.

"I tried to stop her," Micaela went on. "I told her it was definitely not cool to spread rumors. But Darci was into it. I think it's her way of getting attention. She's so desperate to be popular here. I'm really sorry, Ian. The story's going to be all over school by the end of the day. I just thought you should know."

Ian felt his face go scarlet with anger and humiliation. For over a year now, he'd dreaded people finding out about his father. He'd managed to keep it a secret—and then, in a moment of insanity, he'd told Darci. He'd thought he could trust her. How could he have been so wrong?

"Are you okay?" Micaela asked, her voice concerned.

Ian didn't answer. If he tried to talk, he'd start shouting. And then he'd probably yank Darci out of Spanish class and shake her till her teeth rattled.

Instead, he turned away from Micaela and began walking. He didn't know where he was going. Any place that was far away from Northridge. Any place where he wouldn't have to deal with the entire school talking about his father.

He couldn't believe it! He could not believe he'd trusted Darci with his secret, and she'd turned around and broadcast it!

Ian pushed open the door to the parking lot and started outside, only to walk straight into Mr. D'Alonzo, the assistant principal.

"Going somewhere, Mr. Hassler?" the administrator asked.

Ian shut his eyes. He really didn't need this

right now. He knew exactly what would happen. D'Alonzo would give him a lecture, a detention, and a late pass into geometry. Ian would sit in that dumb class, steaming. And he'd think of a way to get back at Darci Callahan.

Darci was feeling good as she headed back to her locker at the end of the day. The trauma of the chemistry disaster had faded. She'd gotten a B+ on a pop quiz in Spanish. She'd even managed to make her lump of clay resemble a cat in art class.

And ever since this morning, she'd been thinking about Ian. He'd asked her out. At least he would have, if she hadn't been so freaked and dashed off to Spanish class. Ian Hassler wanted to go out with her! She couldn't help wondering what it would be like to be Ian's girlfriend, to walk through the halls together, to go on dates together, to kiss good night...

All that day Darci had been hoping she'd run into him so they could finish their conversation.

Darci was halfway to her locker when she stopped. She was pretty sure Ian's locker was next to the wood shop on the first floor. Maybe she ought to go down that hall, just in case he was still there.

Her heart racing with excitement, Darci headed toward the wood shop. Sure enough, Ian was at his locker, cramming textbooks onto a narrow shelf.

"Hi," Darci said.

Ian turned around, looked straight through her as though she didn't exist, then turned back to his locker.

"Ian," Darci said, "I wanted to talk to you about going to a movie later this week."

"You certainly do like to talk, don't you?" he replied in a bitter tone.

"What?"

Ian grabbed a jacket and a notebook and kicked the metal locker door shut. "I've got soccer practice now," he said sharply.

"Fine," Darci said. She knew there was a major game coming up tomorrow, and Ian was the team's star forward. Maybe he was stressed about soccer. "I just wanted to know if you'd want to check out the new twelve-plex this week," she tried again.

"Not with you, I don't," Ian replied.

Darci felt as if she'd been slapped. "I-I don't get it," she said. "This morning you wanted to go out with me. Remember, you asked if I wanted to see a movie. Did I imagine that?"

Ian's voice was perfectly flat as he said, "No, you didn't imagine it."

"Well, what's changed since then?"

"Nothing's changed," Ian said. "Except now I know the truth about you."

"Ian, you've got to tell me what you're talking about," Darci pleaded.

"I don't have to do anything," Ian told her. "Besides, you do enough talking for both of us."

He headed off to the gym without looking back.

Darci bit down on her lip as she watched him go. She wouldn't cry. She wasn't going to let a boy she barely knew hurt her so badly. But her face was hot with humiliation, and she felt as though something deep inside her had been torn in half and would never mend.

CHAPTER 8

"Great practice, dude," John Leone remarked as Ian came into the locker room.

Ian spun open his combination lock, took out his gym bag, and pulled his sweaty soccer jersey over his head.

"Really great scoring," Leone went on. "I particularly liked that move where you passed the ball to the other team. What do you call that—cooperative soccer?"

"Look," Ian said, grabbing a towel from his bag. "The coach just spent fifteen minutes chewing me out. Do you have to rub it in?"

His friend shook his head. "No, I'm just wondering what's wrong. I've never seen you play so lousy. Are you okay?"

Ian rolled his eyes and started toward the showers. "I'm fine."

Leone caught his arm. "No, you're not. What is going on?"

Ian glanced around the locker room. They were the only two members of the team still there. Everyone else had cleared out fast after the disastrous practice.

Ian sat down heavily on one of the wooden benches. "Remember last year I told you about my dad?"

John nodded.

"Well, you're the only person in Northridge that I'd told. Until last week when I told Darci Callahan. Then this morning Micaela James tells me that Darci's spreading the story, and sure enough, everyone's coming up to me to ask me gross questions about what prison's like."

"Micaela…" John said thoughtfully. "Isn't she that witchy girl? The one who did a tarot reading for Phillip's sister. She told her to be careful around cars, and the very next day Sharon was in an accident."

"This isn't about Micaela," Ian said. "It's about Darci and the fact that she can't keep her mouth shut."

"It'll blow over," John said. "Next week they'll all be gossiping about something else."

"Maybe," Ian agreed. "But from now on, everyone's going to think of me as The Kid Whose Father Is in Prison. And I hate it."

Leone was quiet for a moment before saying, "Darci's the one in your history class?"

"Yeah," Ian said in a flat voice. "I thought I liked her."

"So what are you going to do?"

"I don't know." Ian ran a hand through his black hair. "I've considered murdering Darci, but I figure having one member of our family in jail is about all my mother can take right now."

"You could start a counter-rumor," John suggested.

"No, that's too low," Ian said. "I'd be as bad as she is."

"I could ask her out and then dump her," John offered.

Ian winced. "You should have seen her face when I told her I didn't want to go out with her. I cut her in half."

"She deserves it," John said.

"I know," Ian agreed. "She's completely wrecking my life, but…"

"But you don't want to hurt her anymore," John finished for him.

Ian nodded. "Yeah. Great revenge, huh? I must be losing my mind. Or turning into a major wuss."

John slapped him on the back. "I hate to be the one to tell you this, dude, but it's worse than that. You've got it bad for Darci Callahan."

Darci came home after school that day to an empty house. For the first time in a long time, she wished her mom were there. It would be comforting to have a cup of tea with her and talk through the mess with Ian. Unfortunately, her mother was away on business and wouldn't be back until the next day. *Even Kurt might be helpful,* Darci thought. Maybe Ian was just going through guy stuff, and Kurt would be able to make sense of it. But Kurt was out with Kristin. Big surprise.

Darci changed into her nightgown and brewed a pot of spiced tea. She watched TV for a while, made an attempt to do her math homework, and then tried to read. It was no good. She couldn't concentrate on anything when she was depressed. She thought about going to bed, but she knew she was still too upset to sleep.

She had to talk to someone. She went into her mom's room and dialed Micaela's number, hoping it wasn't too late to call.

Micaela picked up on the first ring. "Darci," she said, "I had a feeling it was you."

"How'd you know?" Darci asked.

"I've been working on your chart," Micaela answered. "You're going through some heavy-duty influences now. There's trouble in your fifth house, which relates to matters of the heart."

"What do you mean?" Darci asked.

"According to your chart, romance is rocky for you right now," Micaela explained. "There's a lot of Venus-Mars energy in your stars, which means conflict."

Darci was silent for a moment. It was almost eerie how well Micaela could read her. "Well," she admitted, "Ian Hassler isn't speaking to me anymore."

"Ian's an Aries, a fire sign," Micaela said. "Fire and water don't mix. One destroys the other. His sign and yours can only bring conflict."

"We were getting along just fine," Darci said sadly. "And then suddenly he was furious with me. I don't even know why!"

"Aries is the first sign of the zodiac," Micaela said. "It's the most immature sign, while Pisces is the last sign and the most mature. For you, dealing with an Aries is like dealing with a spoiled, bad-tempered child. Aries is obsessed with the 'I'—they're all totally self-absorbed."

"Ian didn't seem that way at first," Darci said wistfully.

"Well, it didn't take long for his true self to show, did it?" Micaela asked. "Don't worry, Darce, you'll meet someone else. Someone who's much better suited to you."

Darci leaned back against her mother's headboard. "How am I supposed to meet this Mr. Right?" she asked. "Is that in my chart, too?"

"Not yet," Micaela answered. "But let me keep working on it. How's your room coming, by the way?"

"I bought the off-white paint," Darci said. "I just haven't gotten it on the walls yet."

"Why don't I come over tomorrow after school and help you?" Micaela suggested. "We can have a painting party. It'll be fun."

"That'd be great," Darci said.

"See you tomorrow," Micaela said.

"Tomorrow," Darci agreed, hanging up.

She got ready for bed, feeling a little better. She knew Micaela was right. She and Ian probably were never meant to be together anyway.

She and Micaela, though, were a different story.

CHAPTER 9

The next afternoon Micaela arrived at Darci's house dressed in paint-spotted white painter's pants and an open denim shirt over a scoop-neck black leotard. Her hair was pulled back in a French braid. A silver pendant—a bull in a circle—hung at her throat.

"So how's the heartbreak?" Micaela asked as they walked upstairs.

"Mending," Darci answered. "Slowly."

"You'll be fine," Micaela assured her. "I think the universe has some very interesting things in store for you."

"I certainly hope so," Darci replied, leading the way into her room.

"There's no doubt about it," Micaela said. She stepped into the room and quickly appraised the cans of paint and painting supplies. "Okay," she said, "time to get down to business here. Let's push all the furniture to the center of the room, and we'll cover it with a drop cloth. Then we'll put some masking tape on the moldings and start painting."

Darci, who was wearing one of Kurt's shirts and her overalls, began edging her bookcase toward the center of the room while Micaela moved the desk. After making sure that the furniture and moldings were covered, Micaela poured paint into one of the pans and began painting the corners of the room with a brush. "It's best to do the hard part—the corners and the areas near the ceiling and floor—first," she explained. "Then you just use the rollers on the walls. You'll see, we'll be done in a couple of hours."

Following Micaela's example, Darci set to work on another corner of the room. She'd thought painting would be a chore, but it felt great to see the old, grimy sludge blue paint disappear beneath a coat of creamy off-white. "This is excellent," Darci said. "The room feels brighter already."

Micaela nodded. "You're starting to feel your Taurus. You're connecting with that part of you that loves color and material things. That part of you will become more intense as you grow older."

"Do you really see everyone in terms of the zodiac?" Darci asked curiously.

"The zodiac explains a lot," Micaela answered carefully. "And it allows me to predict certain things."

"So you can actually predict the way people will act?"

Micaela began painting the area around Darci's window. Darci noticed that somehow, when Micaela painted, the paint didn't drip at all. "I'm not foolproof," Micaela admitted. "And I can't always predict a person's actions, but if I know someone's sun sign, I have a good idea of what they like and don't like, and what they need."

Darci stepped back, surveyed her paint job, and went back in to touch up some patchy spots. "I think my brother needs a brain transplant," she grumbled. "All he talks about is Kristin. Kurt and Kristin—it even sounds dumb. And when I pointed that out to him this morning—I was just trying to be helpful—he nearly snapped my head off. He said I was just sore because Ian dumped me."

"Were you?" Micaela asked.

"A little," Darci admitted. "But I also think Kurt's getting obsessed with Kristin, and someone has to tell him. I just wish he wouldn't get so grouchy when I do."

"That's the lion," Micaela said. "Hit a sore point and he'll attack. It's not a good idea to piss him off too often."

"Maybe I don't care if he's pissed," Darci said.

"But you do," Micaela told her. "Pisces is a very sensitive sign. You always care what people think of you."

Darci knew Micaela was right. She was miserable when people were angry with her. "What about you?" she asked.

Micaela picked up a roller and began painting one of the walls, working from the center out. "There's this astrologer who says that those who are born under the sign of Taurus have a strong, cool oak tree as their core. So if people don't like me, I just think of that cool oak inside me, and I know it can't be affected by them. Either people like me or they don't. I don't worry about getting anyone else's approval. For anything."

Once again, Darci found herself wishing she were less like an average fifteen-year-old and more like Micaela. Darci knew she didn't have a cool oak inside her. At her core was something that felt more like a shrub. Even though she was still annoyed with Kurt, she couldn't bear to think that he was angry with her. And it drove her crazy that Ian, whom she barely knew, was acting like she'd committed some horrible crime.

Darci heard the sounds of the front door opening and teenage male voices downstairs. Kurt and some of his friends had just come home. "There's the lion now," she said, "probably about to devour everything in the refrigerator."

"Maybe we should go get a snack before he does," Micaela suggested. "We could use a break."

"Okay," Darci agreed. "We can nuke some microwave popcorn."

The two girls went downstairs to find Kurt and two of his friends, Marc Tannenbaum and Eric Close, gathered in front of the microwave and staring at it intently, as though the door was a TV screen. The buttery smell of popcorn filled the kitchen.

Darci rolled her eyes. This time, she decided, the lion was not going to rule. "Kurt," she said, "that last bag of popcorn is mine, and you know it. You already ate the others in that box. So thanks for cooking it for us."

Kurt turned around and his blue eyes widened. "Is that my shirt you're wearing?" he asked. "To *paint* in?"

"You never wear it anyway," Darci pointed out

reasonably. "Besides, you're changing the subject. We were talking about popcorn."

"The shirt is mine and you didn't ask to borrow it," Kurt said.

Darci stepped forward, opened the microwave, removed the bag of popcorn, and poured it into two bowls. "Here," she said. "You guys get one bowl. We get the other."

"Are you joking?" Eric asked. "That's barely enough for *one* of us. We're hungry."

Marc opened the refrigerator. "Don't you people have any food in this house?" he asked in a dismayed voice.

"Not much," Kurt answered, still glaring at his sister. "Darci, go put on one of your own shirts."

"Who died and made you dictator?" Darci shot back. "Stop being so bossy."

"I have an idea," Micaela said. "Let's order in Chinese, my treat."

"Can we have egg rolls, spare ribs, and Mandarin duck?" Eric wanted to know.

"We can order whatever you want," Micaela said, "on one condition: Kurt and Darci call a truce."

Darci looked at her friend in surprise. Was this Micaela's way of getting Kurt to back off?

"Do it, Callahan," Eric said.

"Now," Marc agreed, locking Kurt in a friendly chokehold. "I'm hungry."

With a reluctant sigh, Kurt held out his hand to Darci. "Truce?" he asked.

"Truce," Darci agreed, shaking hands.

Marc released Kurt, and Kurt gave Micaela a rueful smile. "Thanks," he said.

With a minimum of hassle, Micaela put together an order and phoned it in to the Purple Panda. "The food will be here in thirty-five minutes," she reported.

"What do we do until then?" Eric asked, helping himself to a handful of the popcorn.

"We can play a game!" Mark suggested, his voice a parody of an overly enthusiastic camp counselor.

"It's not a bad idea, actually," Kurt said. His eyes went to Darci. "Didn't we just unpack that old Twister game? Remember, Mom wanted to know why we bothered to move it when we never play it."

"I put it up in the attic," Darci said.

"Wise child," Marc said, patting her on the head. "That's exactly where it belongs."

"I'll get it," Kurt offered.

Darci looked at Micaela. It was hard to imagine sophisticated Micaela James doing something as silly as playing Twister. "You up for this?" Darci asked doubtfully.

Micaela shrugged. "Why not? My neck was getting stiff painting. Maybe this will stretch me out."

Kurt came down the stairs a few minutes later, triumphantly holding up the Twister box. He slid a hip-hop CD into the CD player. Then he spread out the game board and set up the dial while Marc and Eric joked around. Darci noticed that while the boys occasionally included her in their teasing, they never included Micaela. In fact, neither of them addressed or even looked at her directly. This struck Darci as very strange. She'd been around Marc and Eric long enough to know that both were extremely popular, and neither was shy around girls. Usually, they both flirted like mad. It wasn't as if they were ignoring Micaela. It was more as if they were keeping a respectful distance.

"I'll spin the dial," Marc volunteered. "Five people are too much for this board."

"You are such a wuss," Eric told him.

"Let him alone," Kurt said. "We'll just make him play the next round."

Marc spun the dial and everyone put their left foot on a red circle.

"Right hand green," Marc called. He spun again. "And now left hand blue."

So far everyone was pretty comfortably positioned.

Then Marc spun "left foot yellow" and "right hand blue." Eric now had his left leg wrapped around Darci's right ankle, and Darci's right hand was crossed over one of Eric's arms. Darci's eyes widened as she saw that Micaela was bent backward in a perfect arch beneath Kurt, who was twisted into a strange position of his own and staring at Micaela with undisguised admiration.

At Marc's next call Micaela, moving as smoothly as a snake, raised her upper body and twisted so that her side was pressed against Kurt's, her breast touching his arm.

Eric craned his neck to watch them, and lost his balance.

"You're out, Close," Marc told him. "We're down to three."

The game continued. Darci was no longer having much trouble placing her hands and her feet, because with each call Micaela made sure that she found a way to press her body against Kurt's; all the action was at their end of the board. Darci watched with amazement. She'd seen a lot of girls come on to her brother, but she'd never seen anything quite like this. Kurt looked as if he wasn't sure what to make of it—his expressions ranged from disbelief to pleasure to frantic attempts to keep his balance.

"Left foot green," Marc called.

This time Kurt was near the ground. He placed his left foot onto a green circle, so that both his feet were stretched in front of him, and his hands were behind him. Micaela placed her left foot on a green circle. Her legs straddled Kurt's hips, her arms were on either side of his shoulders, and her face hovered inches above his. Kurt seemed mesmerized, his concentration fixed on the beautiful girl above him. Both seemed unaware of the others in the room. It was as if they'd entered a private world of their own.

Marc called two more moves. Darci's jaw dropped open as she watched Micaela twist herself around Kurt's body. Her movements were sinuous, and Kurt seemed dazed, lost—as if he'd gone into a place from which there was no return.

"Left foot red!" Marc called.

Kurt stayed perfectly still, frozen, as Micaela slithered around him.

"Kurt!" Darci said, and promptly fell over herself.

"You're out, Darce," Marc announced. He

looked at the two remaining players and shook his head. "I'd say 'You may now kiss the bride,' but"—the doorbell rang—"dinner's here," Marc finished cheerfully. "Game's over, an official tie between Mr. Callahan and Ms. James."

Marc's words seemed to break the trance. Micaela stood up and went to pay for the food. Kurt sank down on the board, looking exhausted and a little shaken.

"That's a mean game of Twister you play," Marc said to Kurt.

"You should definitely go out for a letter in Twister," Eric agreed.

Darci wished the two boys weren't making a joke of it. She was convinced that something serious had just gone on—only she wasn't quite sure what it was.

Darci went into the kitchen, where Micaela was setting the food out.

"I have to talk to you," she said firmly.

"About what?" Micaela asked.

"Upstairs, in my room, now!" Darci insisted.

Micaela looked at her as if she were crazy, but followed Darci upstairs. "All right," she said when Darci had shut the door, "what's so urgent?"

"I want to know what was going on down there with you and Kurt," Darci said.

Micaela brushed back a strand of white-blond hair that had escaped her braid. "I don't know what you're talking about," she said.

"I mean that Twister game," Darci said. "You were all over Kurt. In front of everyone. What *was* that?"

"Darci, I wasn't all over your brother," Micaela said. "*He* was all over me. It's no big deal. You know teenage boys—they can't control themselves."

"I know what I saw," Darci insisted. "You were trying to seduce him."

"I was not," Micaela said calmly. "But what if I was? There's no law against it. Besides, wouldn't you rather have Kurt go out with me than with Kristin?"

"I'd rather have him go out with almost anyone except her," Darci admitted.

"Don't worry about it," Micaela said. "The Twister game didn't mean anything. And as for Kristin—I have a feeling she won't be a problem for long."

CHAPTER 10

Micaela sat in the back of her physics class, paying no attention to Mr. Pendergast's explanation of the second law of thermodynamics. She pulled a small lunar calendar from her purse and glanced at the end of October. Next week there would be a full moon. Sometime before then, she'd have to gather the herbs and stones and incense, draw water from the spring, and make an altar for the scrying dish. Tonight, after her parents were asleep, she would begin the preparations.

She put away the calendar as Mr. Pendergast droned on, and turned her attention to her notebook—which had nothing to do with physics.

She frowned as she reviewed her notes on Hearts of Darkness. Darci's reactions on Saturday had been exactly what she'd expected. Nausea, a little dizziness, the convulsions, and then deep sleep. How much more of the drug, Micaela wondered, would be necessary for hallucinations? For unconsciousness? For eventual slowing of the heart?

She knew the dosages and effects of similar toxins. Chemistry was something she'd intuitively understood since her parents taught her the basics when she was eleven. Since then, with the help of their reference books and computers, she'd gone on and researched her own interests.

But the red powder was still an unknown. And its color a giveaway, unless you happened to have cranberry or grape juice on hand. She'd have to add something to change that. Micaela shut her eyes, forcing herself to recall the dozens of chemical reactions she'd memorized when she first became interested in poisons. She thought of one thing that might neutralize the color. It was a common chemical compound. She could probably find it right here in school.

She shut the notebook with a smile. And as soon as the bell rang, she set off for the chemistry lab.

Ian was halfway to the gym when he realized he'd left one of his notebooks in chemistry class. He swore as he realized he'd have to go back for the notebook. Which meant he'd be late for gym and have to run the track tomorrow morning.

Thoroughly disgusted, Ian turned around and retraced his steps to the chem lab. At least there wasn't a class in there this period, so Mr. Finn wouldn't be there to give him a hard time.

Ian glanced through the open doorway, relieved to spot his notebook still on the desk. He was about to get it when he saw a familiar figure at the very back of the room. Micaela obviously wasn't aware of Ian. She was standing in front of the locked cabinet where Mr. Finn kept the lab chemicals, concentrating on something in her hand.

Wait a minute, Ian thought. *What's Micaela doing here? She takes physics, not chemistry.*

Ian realized that Micaela was breaking into the cabinet.

He watched with amazement as she methodically straightened a paper clip, inserted the wire into the cabinet's lock, and jiggled it. Seconds later the lock snapped open, and Micaela opened the cabinet door. She reached in, removed a small glass jar, and dropped it in her purse. Calmly, she relocked the cabinet.

Ian had seen enough. He ducked into the boys' room and hid out there, giving Micaela time to get out of the lab. After a good five minutes had passed, he returned to the empty chemistry room. He picked up his notebook and stood for a moment in front of the locked cabinet. *What had she stolen?* he wondered. And what was she going to do with it? What exactly was the "strange stuff" that Micaela James was into?

He stood there remembering how quickly she'd picked the lock, how smoothly she'd committed the theft. This clearly wasn't the first time Micaela had stolen something.

So Micaela was a thief. But why steal from the chem lab, of all places? If you were going to steal something, you might as well take something valuable, like a CD player. The fact that Micaela had broken into a locked cabinet for a chemical was just weird enough to be a little scary.

Ian started back toward the gym, still wondering about what he'd seen. *She's a thief,* he told himself. His long experience with his father immediately gave him a second piece of information. *If she's a thief,* Ian realized, *then it's a sure bet she's also a liar.*

Darci was on her way out of school that day when Ian ran toward her. "Darci, wait up!" he called. "I have to talk to you!"

Darci was half-tempted to keep walking. What

if he just wanted to hurt her again? But she slowed, her heart pounding.

"What do you want?" she asked when he caught up with her.

"I've got to talk to you for a few minutes," Ian said.

"I thought you never wanted to talk to me again."

"I'm sorry," Ian said. "I made a big mistake. I think we were set up." He gestured toward one of the big chestnut trees on the side of the school. "Let's sit down for a few minutes, and I'll explain. Please?"

Reluctantly, Darci followed him. Sitting outside the school with him made her heart ache. It reminded her of that first sweet lunch they'd had together.

"The reason I got so mad at you was that Micaela came up to me that day and told me that you'd been spreading the word all over school about my father," Ian began.

"What?" Darci said. "I didn't tell anyone"—her voice faltered—"except Micaela."

"That's what I just figured out," Ian said. "Earlier today I saw her steal something from the cabinet in the chem lab."

Darci shook her head. "I don't get it. What's

that got to do with anything?"

"She broke into that cabinet like a pro," Ian explained. "That wasn't the first time she'd stolen. If she's a good thief, then she's probably also a liar. I think *she's* the one who told the entire school about my father and then blamed you for it. I'm sorry I believed her. I should have at least asked you if what she said was true."

"You should have," Darci agreed. Her voice softened. "I'm sorry I told her about your dad. But I can't really believe Micaela would do that. She's not the type to gossip."

"Unless there's a reason," Ian said. "I think she did it deliberately to break us up."

"That's crazy!" Darci said. "Why would she want to do that?"

Ian leaned back against the tree. "I don't know," he admitted. "I don't understand the first thing about Micaela James. But I do know she's witchy enough to have scared off half the school. I mean, don't you think it's strange that Micaela's so talented and smart and beautiful, and you're the only person who actually talks to her?"

"She's different," Darci said, wanting to defend her friend. "She's a lot more sophisticated than most kids in this school. So she doesn't really fit in."

"That's the understatement of the year!"

Darci thought for a moment. "Micaela thinks that we're not good for each other because of our signs. That you being an Aries and me being a Pisces—we can only cancel each other out."

"And you believe that?" Ian asked.

"I don't know," Darci said. "She's been right about a lot of things. She's kind of psychic. Besides, you did really hurt me."

Ian groaned and shut his eyes. When he opened them again, he looked directly into Darci's eyes. "I've got an idea," he said. "Neither one of us really knows what the story is on Micaela. So let's just wait and see what happens. I want us to be friends." He held out his hand to Darci. "Deal?"

Darci thought it over for just a second before placing her hand in his. "Deal," she said. She started to shake hands and was surprised when Ian pulled her toward him and kissed her lightly on the lips.

"Oh," she said. Ian's kiss made her feel light and happy, as if everything inside her were spinning.

"I think," Ian said slowly, "that we may have to call off that deal right now."

"What do you mean?"

Ian was smiling at her, his eyes light with

warmth. "I think," he said, "that you and I may wind up being more than friends." And then he kissed her again.

Micaela took a small wooden box from her chest of drawers and opened it. Inside were twelve rusted nails she had taken from the graveyard. It had terrified her to go into the cemetery on the night of the full moon and unearth the old coffin. She'd dug for hours, her hands blistered, her shoulders aching. She remembered the smell as the shovel hit the moldering wooden box. She remembered how her hands had trembled as she'd pulled the nails out one by one. And yet she had no regrets. Certain things were necessary for certain spells.

She's with him again.

Micaela straightened up, her hand closing over the rusted nails. Had she really heard that? No, she told herself, it had to be her imagination. The voice only came to her in dreams.

Darci's with Ian again. He'll turn her against you. You must act now.

This time there was no mistaking it. She'd know that voice anywhere—a woman's voice, low and commanding and resonant with centuries of power. Giving her power.

Micaela felt herself trembling with excitement. The voice had come to her while she was awake. It was no dream. It was as real as the rusted nails she held in her hand.

You must act now to stop them.

"I will," Micaela vowed aloud. "By sun, moon, and stars, by the power of the darkness, I swear I will."

CHAPTER 11

Micaela waited three days to obey the voice. The spell to break up Darci and Ian had to be cast on Saturday, when the influence of the planet Saturn was most powerful.

Late on Saturday afternoon, one hour before the sun was due to set, Micaela began her preparations. First, she dressed in a simple black floor-length tunic. Except for a sapphire ring, she wore no adornments. She lit myrrh incense, letting the heavy scent fill the room, calling on the planets to aid her in this ceremony.

Next she set a small wooden table in the center of her room and covered it with midnight blue velvet. On the fireplace mantel and on the table she lit black candles. Blue and black were the colors sacred to Saturn. In the center of the table she placed a curved, silver-bladed knife, next to a small bronze urn that she used as her cauldron. She set a piece of charcoal in the urn, lit it, and placed the hemlock and hellebore on it.

Micaela went to the Chinese cabinet and opened the drawer containing the midnight blue silk pouch. She set the pouch in the crescent created by the knife's blade. Two more objects were needed: a stick of soft beeswax and a silver heart charm, taken from her own charm bracelet. When everything was ready, Micaela turned off the lights in the room and knelt in front of the altar. She concentrated on the rhythm of her breath, clearing her mind of all thoughts and all distractions, of everything but the task before her.

Just as the sun began to set and dusk began, Micaela spoke aloud, "Saturn, planet who sets obstacles and binds, ruler of limitations and death, I ask that you answer my summons and aid me now."

Taking the beeswax in her hand, Micaela began to work it and shape it, until it took on Darci's shape. From the silk pouch she took the lock of Darci's hair.

Using the silver blade, she cut the lock of brown hair in half. Half she carefully attached to the head of the wax figurine. Half she bound with blue embroidery floss. Finally, she took the silver heart-shaped charm and strung it around the neck of the wax doll. Micaela gazed at the doll with satisfaction. It was a good representation of Darci, cruder than the sculpture but as easy to recognize.

She was ready to begin. She took the bound lock of hair from the altar and began to speak: "With this offering, I ask you to bind Darci Callahan's will to my own. Let her have no thought, no desire, that I would not will. Let any part of her that would defy me meet with insurmountable obstacles. Let Darci Callahan be mine."

She set the lock of hair in the urn and touched the candle to it. The smell of burning hair mingled with the scent of myrrh. The sun was almost gone now, and the room dark. The candles threw eerie, flickering shadows against the walls.

Micaela picked up the wax figurine. She touched the silver heart that hung around its neck. "Hear me, Saturn," she said. "This night Darci Callahan gives her heart to another. But she must be mine to mold and shape, mine to recreate."

With a violent jerk, Micaela ripped the silver heart from the doll and threw it in the burning urn. "Let her love for Ian Hassler be destroyed. May the very thought of him be as painful to her as walking through flame." She added more hellebore and hemlock to the fire. "May the love she bears him be poisoned by my hate."

Micaela began to work the wax again, stretching it, compressing it, folding it until Darci's form was unrecognizable. "Let Darci Callahan be mine," she chanted. "I shall teach her, train her, shape her to do my will and the will of darkness."

Micaela remained kneeling as darkness fell and the candles flickered out. She was rewarded for her efforts. As the sun dipped below the horizon the voice returned, clear and strong,

You have done well. All that you asked for, you shall have.

Darci shivered a little as the last rays of light faded from the sky. In front of her, the Hudson stretched out like a broad dark ribbon. Beside her, Ian held her hand in his. It was Saturday evening. That afternoon they'd gone skating with some of Ian's friends and then out for ice cream. Afterwards, Darci had been surprised when Ian offered to walk her home. "In about a week it'll be too cold to walk along the river," he'd explained. "Let's do it now while we still can."

So Darci and Ian were walking the four miles from his house to hers. Darci wouldn't have minded if they walked ten miles. Being with Ian felt good and right and wonderful.

"Sometimes I like to come down to the river at night and listen to the sounds the water makes," Ian said. "It's different every time."

Darci wished this day would never end. "Maybe we should just stay out here," she suggested.

"I thought your mom wanted you home by seven tonight."

Darci rolled her eyes at the reminder. "She does. See, she's making a big deal about curfew because she's sure that when she's away, Kurt and I stay out much later."

"Do you?" Ian asked.

"Of course we do," Darci said with a laugh. "Wouldn't you?"

"Even when my mom's there, I'm always sneaking out," Ian confessed. "She says my problem is I have a hard time following other people's rules."

"Do you?"

"Definitely," Ian replied.

"Micaela would say that's typical of an Aries," Darci told him. "Aries guys need to overthrow the old rules and bring in new ones of their own."

"Micaela again," Ian said softly. "I take it you two are still friends."

Darci didn't want to argue with Ian. She just

wanted him to understand. "When I'm with Micaela, I feel like I've entered another world," she explained. "We talk about things like fate, things that most people don't even think about. Sometimes I think Micaela knows me better than anyone else."

"Maybe I ought to study up on fate," Ian murmured. He leaned forward and kissed Darci lightly on the forehead.

Darci moved into his arms and tilted her face up to his. Ian's mouth met hers in a kiss that sent a rush of warmth straight through to the soles of her feet.

Totally happy, Darci closed her eyes and gave herself up to the moment—and then abruptly pulled away.

"What's wrong?" Ian asked.

Darci shook her head, unable to find words to answer him.

"Did I do something I shouldn't have?" Ian asked, his voice concerned. "I didn't hurt you, did I?"

"It-it isn't anything like that," Darci stammered, her voice trembling.

"Well, then what is the matter?" Ian asked, a trace of irritation in his voice. He sighed and put his hands on her shoulders. "Please, Darce," he said in a gentler tone, "talk to me. Tell me what happened."

Darci found herself struggling to break away from his grasp. "G-get your hands off me!"

Ian's hands flew up in a gesture of surrender. "Okay, I'm not touching you. Now will you please tell me what's bothering you?"

Darci turned away from him and faced the water. She took deep breaths, trying to calm herself, trying to understand. At last she said, "I don't know what happened. All I know is that one minute I was kissing you and everything was great. And the next it felt—"

"Wrong?" Ian guessed. "Did your mom tell you that you're not supposed to let guys kiss you or something?"

Darci shook her head. "It's nothing like that. And the feeling was much stronger than that." She took another breath before continuing. "Ian, it felt like there was suddenly a wall of fire between us. And if I touched you or even went toward you I'd be burned so bad—"

"It's my fault," Ian said. "It's because I dumped you before. You're scared you'll get hurt a second time."

Darci whirled on him furiously. "Will you stop trying to explain it away?" she shrieked. "I just told you what happened. What I felt was much worse than being afraid you're going to hurt me. It was literally like having a wall of fire blazing between us. About to kill us both. Don't you understand?"

"No," Ian said. "I don't."

Darci bit her lip to keep from crying. "Then I'll explain it to you," she said. "I don't know why it happened, but I do know what it means. I can't see you again."

"But we just had a great day together," Ian protested, stepping toward her.

Darci backed away from him, terror in her eyes. "Stay away from me," she hissed. Then she turned and ran the rest of the way home.

CHAPTER 12

Kurt came out of school on Monday afternoon to find Micaela leaning against his van. A light rain was falling beneath a heavy gray sky. Micaela stood in the rain, dressed in a short black slip-like dress that showed through a transparent raincoat. She wore sheer black stockings and black heels. Kurt couldn't believe they actually let her get away with wearing something like that to school. Then again, he had a feeling that Micaela got away with a lot of things that no one else did.

"Hey," he said, trying to sound casual. Ever since that bizarre Twister game, Kurt had been wondering what the story was with Micaela. Had that been a come-on? He hadn't heard from or talked to her since then. Besides, she knew he was seeing Kristin. "Are you looking for Darci?" he asked.

"Actually, no," Micaela said. "I was looking for you. My car's starter just died. The engine won't turn over at all. I was wondering if maybe you could give me a ride home."

"Sure," Kurt said, surprised at the request. "But I've got jumper cables in the van. Maybe it's the battery. Why don't you let me try to jump it first?"

Micaela shook her head, long white-blond hair flying in the wind. "No, it's definitely the starter," she said. "It's happened before. I already called my mechanic. He's going to tow it to the garage. All I need is a ride home."

Kurt eyed the brand-new silver Acura sitting a short distance away. "My van may be pretty funky compared to your car."

Micaela stepped up to him and ran a cool hand down the side of his face. Beneath the overcast skies her eyes seemed a strange bright green, like a cat's eyes, glowing with an inner fire. "Do you really think I care about that?" she asked him in a soft voice.

Kurt didn't know how to answer, because he was sure that the question she was asking had nothing to do with the words she was speaking.

"You and I have never really gotten a chance to know each other," Micaela went on. Now her hand rested on his chest, just above his heart. "Maybe it's time we did."

"Yeah," Kurt said, trying to slow his racing heart. He turned and opened the door of the van. "Climb in," he said, trying to keep his voice sounding normal. "I'll take you home."

"What if I don't want to go home?" Micaela asked, her voice mocking.

The rain started to come down harder, but Kurt barely noticed. He couldn't take his eyes off Micaela.

"Where do you want to go then?" he asked.

"I want to take you somewhere," Micaela said, her voice a whisper. "Let me show you." She reached up with both hands, drew his head down to hers, and pressed her lips against his.

Kurt let himself get lost in the kiss. He had no choice. Micaela seemed as irresistible a force as the ocean.

Until he remembered an exquisite girl with long red hair.

Kurt's hands shot out, thrusting Micaela away. "I-I can't do this," he stammered.

"Why not?" Micaela asked in a cool voice. She reached for him again, her hand closing on his wrist.

"Because." Gently, Kurt detached his hand from hers and backed away. "Because of Kristin."

Micaela's eyes flashed. "Kristin?" she asked in disbelief. "She owns you, doesn't she? I thought the lion didn't let anyone else rule him."

"She doesn't own me or rule me," Kurt said. "I love her." He took a deep breath, steadying himself. "I'll give you a ride home if you want. But only a ride."

Micaela's green eyes were no longer focused on him, but on something behind him. Kurt's heart sank as he turned and saw Kristin striding toward them, her face a mask of anger. How much had she seen?

"Hi, Kristin," Micaela said quickly. "Kurt just offered me a ride home. Do you want to ride with us? I mean, it might be a little crowded with three in the van, but—"

"Kris, it's not like that—" Kurt started.

"Oh, no?" Kristin asked. "I suppose you're going to tell me you weren't just kissing her."

"Micaela's car broke down," Kurt said, determined to be honest. "And—"

"Whatever gave you that idea?" Micaela broke in. "My car's just fine." She looked at Kristin. "If I were you, I'd keep a better watch on my boyfriend. That is, if he's still your boyfriend."

"Micaela!" Kurt said. "You said—"

Micaela turned, crossed the parking lot to her

car, started it up without a problem, and drove off.

"Yeah, I can see her car is in really bad shape," Kristin said furiously.

Kurt ran a hand through his hair in exasperation. "Look," he said, "it's not what you think. Why don't we get out of the rain and I'll explain—"

"Don't bother," Kristin said, and left him standing there in the rain.

Thoroughly disgusted, Kurt got into the van. He was going to have to let Kristin cool down— which could take some time. He didn't blame her for being hurt and thinking he was a jerk. Maybe if he brought her some flowers or something, she'd listen long enough to let him straighten things out. He was about to pull out of the school parking lot when a beat-up Ford pulled alongside him. Ian Hassler leaned out the Ford's window. "I saw that whole little scene," he said. "Micaela really pulled a number on you. God, she's smooth."

Kurt glared down at him. "You know, this is none of your business, Hassler."

"I know," Ian said, sounding apologetic. "But I thought that when you do get Kristin to listen to your side, you might want someone to back you up."

Kurt relaxed a little. "Thanks," he said.

Ian started to roll his window up, then stopped. "How's Darci?" he asked.

"I thought you two were back together," Kurt said.

"That's what I thought, too," Ian said. "She hasn't talked to me since Saturday, and I don't even know why."

Kurt looked up at the darkening skies. "Maybe this just isn't a good week for relationships."

"Now you sound like Darci," Ian said. "Next you'll tell me the stars are out of line or something."

Kurt shook his head. "I'm not blaming anything on the stars. It's probably just hormones."

"Or Micaela James," Ian said as he drove off.

CHAPTER 13

On Tuesday after school Darci was in her room, doing homework, when she saw Micaela's car pull into the driveway. Darci hadn't talked with Micaela since last week's Twister game. Or since Ian had told her about Micaela setting them up. She wasn't sure what to make of that. She'd seen Micaela in art class, but Micaela had been preoccupied, totally absorbed in a painting. And Darci hadn't really talked much with anyone since Saturday's strange incident with Ian. She was still trying to figure that one out. She went to the door, wondering if Micaela was angry with her.

"Hi," Darci said a little uneasily. "What's up?"

Micaela didn't look angry at all. She was wearing a long, close-fitting black dress with a tiny flower print. "I finished your chart and thought you'd want to see it," she said.

"Really?" Darci asked, feeling pleasantly surprised. "This really strange thing happened this weekend. Maybe my chart will explain it. Come on upstairs."

"Is your brother home?" Micaela asked as they passed the closed door to Kurt's room.

"He's studying for a calculus exam," Darci said, leading the way into her room.

"This place looks great," Micaela said approvingly.

"Thanks to you," Darci said. It felt good to have Micaela visit again.

"I brought you a present," Micaela said. "It's nothing major," she added quickly. "Just a little something I outgrew." She reached into her pack and pulled out a floor-length green velvet dress.

"It's gorgeous!" Darci gasped.

"Try it on," Micaela urged her. "It doesn't fit me right anymore—it comes up above my ankles."

Eagerly, Darci tried on the dress. Her eyes widened as she saw her reflection in the mirror. The dress made her look sophisticated and exotic like Micaela. "I've always wanted something like this," she murmured.

"It looks good on you," Micaela said. "It suits you." She looked at Darci thoughtfully. "It's the new you."

Darci turned to her, questioning. "Does my chart say something about me changing?"

"Let's see," Micaela said, taking out the chart. "Well…I see what the problem is with Ian. It's your fifth house. You need to be cautious right now—especially with romance. It's very easy for the fish to be overwhelmed and absorbed by another personality. There's danger in losing your heart. In fact, this month the danger will become particularly intense. The fish is far too accommodating for her own good."

"So what should I do?"

Micaela searched the chart for an answer. "You have to be on guard," she said at last. "Protect your heart. Keep a wall around you and don't let your emotions lead you. Above all, avoid romance. You can't trust it. If a guy acts interested, that's a sign from the universe that he's someone you should keep at a distance."

Darci leaned back against her headboard, totally depressed. "Ian and I got back together last week. We had a really nice day together Saturday. And then, Saturday night, I bolted from him. I don't even know why. All I know is something inside me won't let me get near him."

"Trust it," Micaela said. "It's your intuition protecting you. From the first day I met you, I had this feeling about you—I think you may be very psychic, and that's what you're experiencing now."

"Me, psychic?" Darci asked with a laugh.

Micaela nodded. "You just have to learn how to work with those psychic energies. Then there's an amazing amount of information they can give you. It's how I can always guess someone's sign." She looked at the chart again. "There are a lot of good things waiting for you, Darce, as long as you don't let romance pull you down. If I were you, I'd just cool things with Ian. At least until this next Venus transit. If he really cares about you, he'll wait."

Darci rolled her eyes. "Somehow I can't see asking Ian if he'll stay on hold until my next Venus transit."

Micaela stood up and went over to the windows. "If you want to come into your own power, you have to be prepared to make sacrifices," she said slowly.

"What do you mean?" Darci asked.

Micaela turned to face her. "There are a lot of things you can control, Darci. You can learn to work with the elements, to call on the energies of the cosmos. All these things will help you if you know how to summon them."

"I'm not sure I know what you're talking

about," Darci said, but her heart was racing with excitement. Micaela knew so many things; it was as if she held secret upon secret. From the moment she'd seen Micaela's room, Darci had longed to have those secrets opened to her.

Micaela sighed. "I can't explain it. I can only show you. Do you want me to teach you—how to call on darkness and light, how to read the stars, how to draw up the energy of the earth—"

"Yes," Darci said. "That's exactly what I've been wanting all along. I just never really had words for it before."

Micaela smiled. "Good," she said. "But first you have to understand that this is sacred knowledge, not to be transmitted lightly. So we need a pact, you and I. Agreed?"

Darci nodded.

Micaela lit the one candle in Darci's room and turned off the overhead light. "Dusk," she said softly. "It's perfect timing. Now kneel before me."

Darci knelt in the darkened room.

"Repeat these vows," Micaela said. "As day leaves, as night enters, I open my heart to the spirits of earth and sky. I open my eyes to darkness. I give myself to the magic of the elements. I swear to do what is asked of me…"

Darci repeated the vows, her voice trembling.

She didn't know exactly what it was that she was promising—except to enter a new realm, a realm of magic and power where her every thought would be guided by Micaela.

Micaela finished administering her vows to Darci. "Stand up," she said gently. "As of this moment, you are different. The door to your old self and the past is shut. You enter the future as one who wields power."

Darci nodded solemnly and Micaela almost laughed. This was so easy, it was pathetic. Darci had bought the fake horoscope and now she was buying this bogus initiation. Both were important, though, because Micaela wanted Darci to be hers, because the voice had promised that she would be.

"Now what?" Darci asked hesitantly.

Micaela thought for a second. "There are some books you ought to read," she said. "I've got one of them in my pack, which you can start with. They'll give you some background about the skills you're going to learn."

"Great," Darci said.

Micaela took out a book about the history of magic and gave it to Darci. Her mind, though, was on Kurt. Obviously, he hadn't told Darci about the scene in the parking lot yesterday. Micaela visualized him in his room. She could almost feel his presence. She wondered if he felt hers as well. And if he did, was he angry with her? It didn't matter if he was, she told herself. The lion's anger never lasted long.

"Darci," Micaela said suddenly, "didn't you once say that Kurt does all the repairs on his van?"

"He has to," Darci said. "He can't afford a mechanic."

"Do you think he'd mind me asking him a question about my car?"

"Probably not," Darci said. "He never minds being distracted from calculus."

"Be right back," Micaela said. She headed down the hall and knocked on Kurt's door.

"Enter!" Kurt called out. He was at his computer, his back to the door.

Micaela walked up directly behind him and placed a cool hand on the back of his neck.

Kurt sat up straight. "Darci?" he asked in a disbelieving tone.

Micaela was silent.

"Mom?"

"Try again."

He turned, his expression hard. "Micaela," he said. "I don't think you ought to be in my room."

"Please, Kurt," she said. "I want to apologize

for yesterday in the parking lot. I'm sorry I—"

"Forget it," Kurt said. "Just leave me alone and we'll pretend it never happened."

"I can't," Micaela said. "I feel terrible—"

"Then why'd you do it?" he asked angrily. "What was that whole story you made up about your car?"

Micaela shrugged helplessly. "I guess, I just wanted—some time alone with you," she said. "I'm really sorry. It's just that I-I'm really attracted to you, and I didn't know how else to tell you. Or show you."

Kurt sighed. "I can think of a lot of ways that would have caused less chaos in my life."

"Are things any better between you and Kristin?" Micaela asked sympathetically.

Kurt grimaced. "She's still not talking to me."

"She probably wants to make up with you," Micaela assured him. "Scorpios always try to hide their feelings, especially when they're hurt. It's typical of a Scorpion to retreat into silence."

"Is that what explains it?" Kurt asked, sounding tired.

Micaela sat down on the edge of his desk, one leg touching his. "I liked kissing you," she said simply.

For the first time Kurt smiled. "I liked kissing

you, too," he said. "But right now I'm committed to Kris."

Micaela nodded, pressing her leg against his. Kurt's eyes met hers, questioning. Micaela stared into his eyes, willing him to forget Kristin, willing him to want her. She reached out her hand to him.

Kurt put his hand in hers—and then drew it back as though he'd been burned. "I can't," he said. "Kris—"

Micaela put a finger to his lips, silencing him. "It's all right," she said gently. "You don't have to explain. You don't have to do anything right now. Things will work out exactly as they're meant to. It was written in the stars long before we were born. Trust me." She left the room, flashing him a dazzling smile.

CHAPTER 14

Darci was curled up in bed, reading the book Micaela had given her when her mother came in to say good night.

"What are you reading?" Mrs. Callahan asked curiously.

"Nothing," Darci said. She had a feeling that it would not be a good idea to tell her mom about Micaela and the ceremony she'd just gone through.

Her mother raised one eyebrow as she saw the title of the book. "Nothing, huh?" She sat down on the edge of Darci's bed. "You know, when I was your age I was into magic, too. Actually, I thought I was some sort of witch."

"You?" Darci nearly dropped the book in astonishment. The last thing in the world she could imagine was her practical, efficient mother practicing witchcraft. "You've got to be kidding!"

Mrs. Callahan gave her daughter an indignant look. "I don't know why the idea is so incredible to you. I was quite serious about it."

Darci started laughing. "Sorry, Mom," she said, "but you just don't seem like the type to me."

"And you are?"

"Maybe," Darci said. "I feel different lately. Like everything is changing, and I'm entering a new stage of my life."

"You are," her mother said softly. "You're growing up."

"That's not what I mean," Darci said. "I feel things I've never felt before. I want different things, like—"

"Power?" her mother guessed.

Darci nodded.

"You know, there are all sorts of power. And when you're fifteen and still living at home, having to do what your mother tells you and what your teachers tell you—well, then magic can seem quite seductive."

Darci held up the book. "You're going to tell me this is all nonsense, right?"

"No," her mother said. "I think magic is real."

Mrs. Callahan kissed Darci on the forehead and stood up. "I just don't think you need witchcraft, honey. I think you're more powerful than you realize."

That night Micaela entered her secret garden. She'd given Kurt a chance to come to her freely. He'd even admitted that he wanted her. And still Kristin was in the way.

Micaela was tired of waiting. The full moon bathed the garden in silver light. The night skies were with her. Tonight, she would remove all obstacles from her path.

She stepped into the very center of the circle of death camas, a green wool cloak draped around her unclothed body. It was midnight, the dividing line between one day and the next, the time that belonged neither to the day that had passed nor the one to come, the time when it was easiest to call on the unseen energies.

Micaela let the cloak fall to the ground and raised her bare arms to the night sky. As she had done so many times before, she called on the four elements and the four directions, the heavenly bodies, the energies that drove thunder and rain, lightning and wind. And the darkness. She summoned the darkness to do her will.

She took Kurt's leather choker, the one she had stolen from his room the very first time she'd been in his house. She ran a finger along the leather, along the glass bead. She could almost feel the warmth of Kurt's skin as he'd worn it. She had only to touch the smooth bit of glass to feel his presence.

Holding the choker in one hand, she knelt and dug a hole with the other. Gently she set the choker in the hole, then set one of the Hearts of Darkness seedlings over it.

"May his heart grow in love for me as these Hearts of Darkness grow," she chanted. "Let him love me and no other. May his heart be mine for all time. With death camas as my witness, let Kurt Callahan be mine until death."

Once the choker was planted beneath the Hearts of Darkness, Micaela still had one more task in the garden.

She knelt before the shrine she had created. The base was a rock, a flat water-carved oval piece of granite she'd found up in the mountains. On top of it was a round silver dish.

She reached into the deerskin pouch at her side, and took out a bit of coral. "An offering of the earth to the night," she murmured. "I call on the dark to open a window into the future and show me what I must do."

Carefully, she took the crystal pitcher filled

with water from the mountain spring and poured water into the shallow silver dish. She set the pitcher down and gazed into the water. The moon's reflection shone back at her, a cold white sphere against a black sky.

"Open the future to me," she whispered. "I call on you to show me what I must do and remove all obstacles from my path."

A sacrifice was necessary. Micaela reached for the curved bone-handled knife. Without flinching, she drew the blade across her wrist and let three drops of blood fall into the silver scrying dish.

The moon's reflection in the water began to waver. It became brighter and then suddenly darker. And then the reflection of the moon disappeared altogether and was replaced by the image of Kristin Harper. Kristin standing in the woods, walking uncertainly, as if searching for something. Kristin walking and then suddenly vanishing. It was as if Kristin had suddenly been sucked into the darkness.

Beneath the October moon Micaela watched the scene impassively. The woods remained; the girl was gone. She didn't understand what she saw, and yet she knew that in time she would.

She rocked back on her heels, letting the image

in the scrying dish fade. She pulled the cloak around her, still puzzling over the image.

"Tell me," she whispered to the night. "Tell me what I must do. I'll do whatever's necessary, I swear it."

This time the voice spoke, clearer than ever.

Kurt Callahan will be yours. But first you must give Kristin Harper to the darkness."

CHAPTER 15

Micaela paced her room restlessly.

She knew how to give Kristin to the darkness.

She'd begun the preparations two nights ago, as soon as the voice had spoken to her. What she still didn't know was how to lure Kristin into her trap. Every plan she came up with seemed terribly complicated. And long ago, Micaela had learned that the best plans were simple ones. The fewer the details, the less the chance of failure.

She considered sending Kristin a note, forging Kurt's handwriting, but that would mean stealing something with his writing already on it and she couldn't risk that. Now that she'd cast the love spell on Kurt, it was important that he trust her.

Micaela drew the curtains in her room and began lighting candles. She would do what she always did when she was stuck. She'd ask the energies that guided her for help.

Standing in the center of the dimly lit room, Micaela concentrated on her breath until all her thoughts were gone, until there was only endless darkness stretching out all around her.

"Earth and sky, planets and stars, light and the everlasting darkness, I call on you," she began. "I need your aid. I will gladly give Kristin Harper to the darkness as you asked, but—"

Her words were cut off by the return of the voice.

Call her.

"Call her?" Micaela echoed.

Call and I will be with you.

Micaela felt a slight chill against her arm, and knew that the voice was gone. It was more than a voice now. It was a physical presence. And when it left, it always left her feeling empty—as though she'd lost something precious she might never experience again.

What did it mean by *call her*? Micaela stood for a moment, calling Kristin with her mind. She knew at once that wouldn't work. She had to be closely connected to someone to reach them psychically. She could reach Darci that way, but not Kristin.

That left what—the phone? Micaela shrugged.

Stranger things had been asked of her. She picked up the phone book, found Kristin's number, and dialed. She had no idea what she'd say. But she trusted the voice.

She waited as the phone rang once, twice, three times. Kristin picked it up on the fourth ring. "Hello?" she said, her voice already impatient.

"Kris." Micaela stared at the receiver in her hand, the hair on the back of her neck rising. It wasn't her own voice speaking. *It was Kurt's.*

"Are you taking a break from your fling with Micaela?" Kristin asked in acid tones.

"Kris, it's not like that." Micaela gave into the voice, let it say whatever it wanted. "Look, I know what you saw, and I'm sorry. It's not going to happen again. I swear, it's you I'm in love with, not Micaela."

Kristin yawned into the phone. "Could have fooled me," she said in a bored tone.

"Let me prove it to you," Kurt's voice said. "Tomorrow night. I've got something really special planned. I've found this place in the woods. It's really beautiful. No one else knows about it. It'll be just you and me. Will you meet me there? Please?"

Micaela's heart beat hard as Kristin hesitated. What if she refused?

"I'll make it all up to you," the voice promised.

"All right," Kristin said at last. "I'll see you tomorrow and give you one more chance. But that's it."

"Great!" the voice said eagerly. "Listen, I want to get there early and set things up. So this is where you should meet me…"

Five minutes later Micaela hung up the phone. She was trembling. She couldn't believe what had just happened. The voice had not only directed her, it had taken over, changed her own voice into Kurt's. It was getting more powerful by the day. What, Micaela wondered, would it have her do next?

Micaela wiped sweat from her forehead and glanced at her watch. It was so dark, she could barely make out the numbers. Not only was the sky overcast and the moon waning, but she was standing in the bottom of a narrow pit about seven feet below the surface of the earth. It was just past nine. If her plan worked, Kristin would be here in forty minutes.

Micaela leaned against the shovel and caught

her breath. For the last three nights, she'd driven out here and worked till her arms were too tired to lift the shovel. Fortunately, the ground was soft. On every side, damp earth walls rose straight over her head. Kristin was a little shorter than she was, Micaela calculated. The pit ought to hold her nicely. It was time to cover it up.

A thick rope whose other end was tied to a tree hung down inside the pit. Micaela tied the shovel to its end. Then she grabbed the rope and began to climb out of the pit. She slipped a few times, but she held on and kept climbing.

She pulled herself out and took a deep breath, feeling the cold night wind against her skin. It felt good to be out of the pit. She hadn't even admitted to herself how scary it was to be down there.

Micaela pulled up the rope and the shovel. She set the shovel aside, untied the rope from the tree, and put that aside too. Then she smoothed out the mounds of earth on the sides of the pit. Moving quickly, she began to cover the top of the pit with loose brush.

A short while later she surveyed her work, satisfied. In the dark no one could tell that there was a pit beneath the casual scattering of branches and leaves.

Carefully, she hid the shovel and rope. She lit a

candle lantern. On the side of the pit farthest from the road she set out a picnic blanket with an empty picnic basket, a bottle of wine, an empty envelope with Kristin's name on it, and a vase of flowers.

Maybe the flowers were too much? No, she decided. Kurt was trying to win Kristin back. Flowers were appropriate. She set the lantern on the picnic blanket, and then lit three other lanterns, which she placed along the path that led to the pit. Finally, she hid herself behind a tree just across from the pit.

Tonight the scorpion would be claimed by the earth. And she'd be there enjoying every second of it.

Twenty minutes later, Micaela heard a car pull off the road. Kristin.

She listened for the sound of the car door opening and shutting.

Kristin should be finding the two stone gateposts and the footpath about now. She would be walking slowly, afraid of the dark.

She waited silently, calculating that Kristin should be approaching the first of the three lanterns. The wait was almost unbearable. What if Kristin managed to walk around the pit instead of across it? Then she'd find an empty picnic basket and envelope and realize she'd been stood up by her date. That would, of course, make Kristin even angrier at Kurt than she already was. But that wasn't enough. Kristin had to follow the plan.

At last Micaela heard footsteps. She peered out cautiously. It was Kristin, all right, dressed in a denim jacket and one of her baby doll dresses. Kristin was walking slowly. She seemed a little frightened by the woods, but also intrigued. She looked exactly the way she had in the scrying dish.

Micaela held her breath as Kristin entered the clearing and saw the picnic spread. "Oh, Kurt!" came her whisper.

Go ahead, Micaela urged her silently. *Go pick up the envelope.*

"Kurt?" Kristin called to the dark woods. She was shivering, uncertain. "Kurt, where are you?"

Pick it up! Micaela commanded silently. *Go get the envelope.*

Hesitantly, Kristin started toward the picnic blanket. Micaela smiled as the sharp snap of breaking branches followed by Kristin's high-pitched scream filled the clearing. A second later Kristin screamed again as she hit the bottom of the pit.

Micaela sagged against the tree in relief.

"Thank you," she murmured to the darkness and the spirits of the night. "Thank you for helping me."

She stood awhile, listening as Kristin screamed herself hoarse. She called for Kurt, cursed him, pleaded for help from anyone who might be passing by.

Micaela went to stand at the side of the pit and shone a flashlight down. Kristin was covered with dirt but seemed otherwise unharmed.

"Kurt isn't here," she told her prisoner. "He never was. In fact, he doesn't even know you're here."

"But he called me," Kristin insisted.

"Did he?" Micaela asked, laughing as the words came out in Kurt's voice.

"*It was you!* You sick, disgusting—"

Micaela's own voice returned. "I'm afraid I'm the only one who's going to be here tonight, Kristin. You'll just have to deal with me." She knelt by the side of the pit. "Tell you what, Kris. I'll think about helping you out of there if you'll hand up your car keys."

"You're going to steal my car, too?" Kristen shrieked.

"Why are you worrying about a car?" Micaela asked. "What you ought to worry about is whether or not you're ever going to get out of this pit. No one's going to come by. No one knows you're here except me. And I promise you, if you don't hand up those keys, you haven't got a chance."

"You're doing this because you want Kurt."

"Maybe. Maybe not. Even that doesn't matter now. All that matters now is whether you're ever going to see daylight again. Think about it."

Kristin let loose a stream of furious curses followed by more screams. Micaela settled cross-legged by the side of the pit, waiting patiently. At last when Kristin was sobbing quietly she said, "The keys, Kris. Let me have them and you've got a chance."

Still sobbing, Kristin reached into her jacket pocket and handed up her key ring.

"Good girl," Micaela said, reaching down and snatching it. She stood up, went for the shovel, and began to fill in the pit.

Kristin's voice was frantic. "You said you'd help me!"

"I said I'd think about it," Micaela corrected her. "That you'd have a chance. Well, I thought about it and what I think is, the earth would be a much nicer place with you permanently belowground. You took your chance, Kris. Sorry it didn't work out."

Ignoring Kristin's screams, Micaela continued to fill in the pit. It was hard work, but it felt good. It felt better than anything had ever felt.

The pit was just over half full when Micaela stopped. She thought she saw a light at the top of the ridge. In all the years she'd been coming here, she'd never seen anything up there before. She concentrated—there was definitely someone up there. And the last thing she needed was for them to see her.

She looked down. Kristin was buried up to her shoulders. That ought to hold her for a while. Using her hands, Micaela pushed a last mound of earth into the pit. Kristin might not be fully covered, but she wasn't going anywhere, that was for sure. So she'd die of hunger and exposure instead of suffocation. It was all the same in the end.

"Gotta run, Kris," Micaela said. "It's been real."

Kristin didn't answer, but Micaela didn't care. She blew out the lantern on the blanket and scooped up all her props. Next she grabbed the shovel and rope and wrapped them in the blanket as well. She made her way out of the woods, stopping to pick up the other three lanterns.

She smiled as Kristin's Chevy came into sight. She opened the trunk, threw in the blanket, got in, and headed west.

She knew exactly where she was going. Like Kristin's burial, the rest of the night was planned. Micaela would make a quick stop to throw the contents of the picnic blanket in the river. Then she'd continue driving. Forty miles away, there was a nice little drop-off on the side of the road. It was all woods there, and the drop-off went about a hundred feet straight down into a ravine. She'd leave the car in gear, get out, and roll it over the edge.

Then she'd hike three miles out to the highway, where there was a bus stop. The bus probably didn't run more than once every four hours at this time of night, and it would only take her as far as the town next to Northridge, but it was worth all the inconvenience.

She'd be home by dawn.

And no one would ever know.

CHAPTER 16

Darci was still half-asleep, staring into her breakfast cereal, when the phone rang. Mrs. Callahan, dressed for work in a navy wool dress, a silk scarf, and navy blue pumps, picked it up.

Kurt came down the stairs, looking unshaven and irritable. "You riding with me today?" he asked Darci.

"You picking up Kristin?" Darci countered.

"I don't think so," he said. "Kristin and I aren't exactly getting along at the moment."

Their mother gestured for them to be quiet. "...No, this is his mother," she was saying. She listened in silence, her expression growing serious. "Just a minute," she said to the caller.

She covered the receiver and said, "It's Mrs. Harper. She says Kristin went out last night around nine and never came home. Do either of you know where she is?"

Kurt was up at once. "No," he said. "Can I talk to her?"

Mrs. Callahan handed over the phone, and Darci watched her brother earnestly explain that he hadn't talked to Kristin since Monday afternoon, and he had no idea where she was. He hung up the phone a few minutes later, his face white.

"They found her car at the bottom of a ravine about forty miles away from here," he reported in a flat voice. "There was no sign of Kristin. Mrs. Harper thinks I-I had something to do with it. She said when Kristin went out last night, she was going to meet me."

Mrs. Callahan put her hand on his shoulder. "I'll call her back and explain that you and Darci were both here with me last night, unpacking the boxes in the living room."

Kurt's voice was shaking. "Sh-she said the police will be at school. I'll probably have to give them a statement."

"Just tell them the truth," Mrs. Callahan said calmly.

"Mom." Kurt gave her a look of desperation. "It's not me I'm worried about. It's Kristin."

By the time Kurt had driven her to school, Darci

was worried about Kristin as well. The image of the red-haired girl's smashed empty car at the bottom of a ravine was haunting. Had she been kidnapped? Murdered? And why did she tell her parents she was going to meet Kurt when she and Kurt weren't speaking?

Kurt hadn't even crossed the parking lot to the school building when two uniformed police officers approached him. "Are you Kurt Callahan?" the taller of the two cops asked.

"Yes," Kurt answered. His voice was firm, but Darci could tell that he was scared. He was clenching his fists to keep from shaking, and he suddenly looked much younger than eighteen.

"We'd like to ask you some questions about the disappearance of Kristin Harper," the second cop said.

"Sure," Kurt said.

Darci blinked back tears as she watched her brother being led away by the police.

"Hey," said a voice by her side. "What's going on?"

Darci turned to see Ian beside her. Instinctively, she started to back away.

"No, wait, please!" Ian said. "I'm not going to hurt you. Or do anything you don't want me to do. But your brother just got escorted off by the cops, and you look like the sky's about to fall in. I just thought you could use someone to talk to. That's all, I swear it."

Darci hesitated. Something in Ian's voice was cutting through her own instincts to run from him.

"I know what it's like to have someone you love led away by the cops," Ian said gently.

"They're only questioning him," Darci said.

"Why? What's Kurt done?"

"Nothing," Darci said. "He was home with me and my mom last night. But last night Kristin Harper disappeared. She told her parents she was going to meet Kurt, even though they haven't even talked to each other since Monday."

Ian was quiet for a moment. "Kris has got her own car, right? Maybe she just split."

"They found her car in a ravine about forty miles away from here," Darci told him. "They think someone pushed it in there. There wasn't any sign of Kristin."

Ian gave a low whistle of astonishment. Then his eyes darkened with anger. "Wait a minute," he said. "I think I know who the cops ought to be questioning. And it isn't your brother."

"Who?" Darci asked.

"I'll give you one guess," Ian said, starting

toward the school. "Her initials are M.J."

Darci rolled her eyes. "Ian, don't start that again. I know you don't like Micaela but—"

"Darci, this isn't about liking or disliking," Ian said. "I think Micaela is playing a game with really high stakes, and you and I and Kurt and maybe even Kristin are caught in it. And we don't even know what the game is, much less how to play it."

"You're serious, aren't you?" Darci said slowly.

Ian nodded. "I know what it's like to be around people who hide things. And there's a feeling you get just before all those secrets bust wide open—just before all hell breaks loose." He looked at her, his eyes pleading with her to believe him. "I've got that feeling now, and it scares me." Impulsively, Ian took her hand and kissed it. Then, before she could stop him, he ran toward the school.

Micaela was putting her coat in her locker when Ian Hassler suddenly appeared at her side.

"I want to talk to you," he said.

"Speak," Micaela said, not bothering to look at him.

"What did you do with her?" Ian demanded.

"What are you talking about?" Micaela countered.

"The police are questioning Kurt about the disappearance of Kristin Harper. And you and I both know Kurt didn't have anything to do with it." Ian slammed the locker door shut. "Where is she?"

Calmly, Micaela reopened her locker and took out the notebook she needed for first period. "I have no idea. I don't know why you're bothering me."

Ian slammed the locker shut again. "Because I saw that whole little scene you rigged on Monday. You deliberately set up Kurt so that Kristin would see him kissing you. You planned that breakup, and I'd bet everything I own that it was only the first step in your plan. You want Kurt and so you got rid of Kristin, didn't you? And how about breaking into the chem lab the other week? Do you want to explain what that was about?"

Micaela started laughing. "You are one paranoid guy," she told Ian. "Where do you get these ideas? You know, you really ought to apply to the CIA. With all these conspiracy theories, you could have quite a career there. They need lunatics like you. Then again, maybe you're just having a temper tantrum 'cause Darci dumped you."

Ian shook his head. "Forget it, Micaela. That's not going to work. You can't attack me and hope all the questions will go away. They won't. I'm going to keep asking them until I get answers."

"Well, then you're going to be very frustrated," Micaela said. "But then the ram has always been a stubborn one, hasn't he?" She leaned forward, grabbed Ian by the hair, and kissed him hard on the mouth. "You see," she breathed. "It could happen to anyone."

She walked away, leaving Ian standing there, dazed. Her own pulse was beating hard. Not that she was scared of Ian. It was just that she was going to have to get him out of the way. She'd thought splitting him up from Darci would stop his intefering. Clearly not. He'd seen her steal from the chem lab, and his suspicions about Kristin's disappearance were too close for comfort. She'd take care of Ian Hassler today.

At lunchtime, Ian took an empty table at the back of the cafeteria. He'd looked all over for Darci, but Darci was nowhere to be found. He wasn't in the mood to sit at the table with the guys from the soccer team, and it was too cold to eat outside. He unloaded the cola and sandwich from his tray, glad for some time alone. He was still trying to make sense of his encounter with Micaela that morning. He was sure she was involved with

Kristin's disappearance. He just couldn't figure out how.

He looked up, his eyebrows raised in surprise as Micaela herself approached his table, a tray in her hands. She was wearing a long, loose-knit pale gray sweater over ribbed black leggings, black leather ankle boots, and a silver ring set with turquoise and coral.

"Mind if I sit down?" she asked.

Ian bared his teeth at her. "I'd rather eat with a rattlesnake," he said, "but go right ahead. This way I can keep asking you questions you won't answer."

Micaela smiled as she set a salad and iced tea on the table. "At least you're honest," she said.

"Which is more than I can say for you," Ian replied.

Micaela reached across the table for the pepper shaker. "I think you've got a very distorted picture of me," she told him.

Ian shook his head. "Oh, no. Actually, I may be the only person in the entire school who sees you for what you are."

"And what's that?" Micaela asked. She was actually enjoying this. Ian was smart, self-confident, and aggressive—pure Aries, a worthy opponent for the bull. She reached across the table again, this time for the salt. Her hand brushed by Ian's glass.

"A master liar and manipulator, just for starters," Ian answered.

Micaela shrugged comfortably. "At least you give me credit for not being an amateur."

Ian drank some of his soda. "You're also a thief," he went on. "And something a lot worse, though that's the part I'm not sure of."

"Ah," Micaela said. "That's easy." She watched calmly as Ian turned a peculiar shade of green and fought to remain upright. His muscles began to twitch involuntarily, and the whites of his eyes began to show.

She got up from the table and walked over to his side. "That something darker?" she whispered. "Try *murderer*."

CHAPTER 17

Darci left the principal's office, thinking that she'd just about missed her entire lunch period. She wondered if it was too late to get some food. She started up the stairs to the cafeteria and stopped as she saw her brother coming toward her.

"Aren't you supposed to be at lunch?" he asked, speaking loudly because there were sirens in the background.

"I was in the principal's office," Darci told him. "The cops were asking me all these questions about where you were last night. And where I was. They said they already talked to Mom at work. I think they wanted to see if our stories matched."

"Did they?" Kurt asked.

"I guess so," Darci said. "They seemed pretty relaxed by the time they told me I could go." She looked at her brother's worried face. "There hasn't been any word on Kristin, has there?"

Kurt shook his head. "Not that I know of. What the—?"

He and Darci were pushed to the side of the stairway as three people dressed in paramedics' uniforms raced up the stairs.

"That explains the sirens," Darci said.

"First Kristin disappears. Now an ambulance shows up at school," Kurt said. "What is going on here?"

Darci shrugged. "I'm going to get some food before the cafeteria shuts down."

"Okay, see you later," Kurt said.

Darci continued on to the cafeteria. But minutes later she was racing back down the stairs. "Kurt," she yelled as she saw her brother's tall figure turning the corner. "Kurt, wait!"

Kurt stopped. "Now what?"

"It's Ian," Darci gasped. "He's the reason the paramedics are here. Something happened to him in the cafeteria. He looks awful. Please—you've got to take me to the hospital."

"We're both going to get detentions for the rest of our lives when they figure out we left the school to come to the hospital," Kurt told Darci.

They were sitting in one of the hospital waiting rooms. Ian had spent two hours in the emergency room, and was now being transferred to intensive care.

"I just need to see him for a few minutes," Darci told her brother. "Then we can go back to school and I'll tell them it was all my fault."

"Oh, that'll help a lot," Kurt said.

Darci smiled at her brother. "Thanks for bringing me here and staying with me. I really owe you for this one."

"Not really," Kurt told her. "I couldn't concentrate on classes anyway with Kristin missing. At least this is a distraction." He looked at Darci curiously. "So what *is* the story on you and Ian?"

"I don't know," Darci said in a small voice. "We were having a real good time on Saturday, and then it was like something came over me, and I knew I couldn't be near him anymore."

"So what are we doing here now?" Kurt asked.

"I don't know," Darci repeated. "It's like there are two parts of me," she explained to Kurt. "One part of me really likes Ian. And another part thinks I should stay far away from him. But he came up to talk to me this morning, when the cops took you in for questioning, and even the part of me that thinks I should stay away wanted to give him a second chance. Then when I saw him carried out on the stretcher…"

Kurt grinned at her. "It's not all that mysterious, you idiot. You're in love."

Darci punched her brother in the arm and was about to say something sarcastic when a doctor walked toward them. "I'm Dr. Bessen," she said. "Are you the friends of Ian Hassler?"

"That's right," Darci said, standing up. "How is he?"

"Not good," the doctor said. "He seems to be suffering from some sort of poisoning."

"It was probably the cafeteria food," Darci said.

The doctor smiled. "I rather doubt it. What we're seeing isn't the result of typical food poisoning. Ian was having convulsions when he was brought in here. And now his pulse rate is dangerously low. He's conscious but very confused. These are the kind of symptoms we sometimes associate with a toxic dose of a drug."

"Ian doesn't do drugs," Darci said. "I'm sure of it."

Kurt spoke up, asking the question Darci hadn't dared ask. "Is Ian going to make it?"

"Not unless we can figure out what's causing this," Dr. Bessen said. "And figure it out quickly."

"Can I see him?" Darci asked. "Just for a few

minutes? Please?"

The doctor looked reluctant, but said, "All right. Two minutes. No more. He's very weak right now. I'll get a nurse to take you in."

"Thanks," Darci said.

As the nurse led her down the hall, Darci tried to take in what the doctor had said. Ian might be dying. Still, she wasn't prepared for what she saw.

Ian lay in a bed in the intensive care ward. Tubes ran into his nose and out of his arms. His eyes were closed and his skin was ash gray. He looked thinner, weaker, as if something inside him was gone. How could someone who'd been so alive that morning look as though all the life was draining out of him seven hours later?

Darci swallowed hard and walked up to the bed. There was still something in her urging her to get as far from Ian as she possibly could. But she fought it down. "Ian?" she said.

Ian's eyes fluttered open. "Darce."

"How are you doing?" Darci asked, and immediately felt like a jerk for asking such a dumb question.

A ghost of a smile flickered across Ian's face. "Been better," he said. "I feel really strange. Everything's got a yellow aura around it. Even you."

"It's my halo," Darci joked, and realized that was probably the most unfunny thing she could have said. This visit was a disaster. "Maybe I'd better go," she said.

But Ian reached out for her hand. "Darce, I need you to do something for me."

"Anything," Darci said.

"Go to Micaela's house. See if you find anything about poisons."

"What? Are you cr—"

"Please just do it," Ian begged. "She was in the cafeteria with me. I think she put something in my food. No one else believes me."

"Your two minutes are up, miss," the nurse announced loudly. "You'll have to leave now."

"Will you do it?" Ian asked Darci, and something in his voice made her think he might never be able to ask for anything again.

Darci nodded, trying not to cry. "I'll do it," she said seconds before the nurse swept her out of the room.

Kurt met her as she stumbled down the hall, half-blind with tears. He put his arms around her. "Ian's not doing so good, huh?" he guessed.

Darci pulled herself out of her brother's arms and wiped her eyes. "Kurt, I need you to do me another favor," she said. "I need you to take me to

Micaela's house now."

"Just for the record," Kurt said half an hour later as he parked the van in the woods bordering the Jameses's house, "I think this is totally insane. Didn't the doctor tell us Ian was confused?"

"He was pretty clear about this one point," Darci said.

"I still think breaking into Micaela's room is a bad idea."

Darci started toward the great stone house. "I promised Ian I would do it for him. And now I have to do it. That's all there is to it."

"All right." Kurt looked at his watch as they approached the house. "It's two-forty now. If we're lucky we'll have at least half an hour before Micaela gets home from school."

Darci took a deep breath, marched up to the door, and rang the bell. A middle-aged woman with a kind face came to the door. "Are you Devon's nanny?" Darci asked hopefully.

"Yes, and who are you?"

"I'm Stacey," Darci lied. "And this is my boyfriend, Jimmy. He drove me over here. Anyway, I'm in Micaela's art class. I was over here working on a project with her, and I left my book in the library. I keep forgetting to ask her to bring it to school and now it's overdue and—"

"Go have a look," the woman said.

"Thanks," Darci said. "I really appreciate this."

She led Kurt to the library on the ground floor and pretended to search for the book.

"Your boyfriend Jimmy?" her brother asked.

"Shhh!" Darci said. She was listening, waiting for the moment when she was sure Devon's nanny would be distracted. A moment later she heard the woman's soft voice, and then a four-year-old boy loudly demanding to watch TV.

"This way," Darci said, leading the way up the stairs to Micaela's room. She pushed open the door with the carved flower on it, relieved that it wasn't locked.

"Nice room," Kurt whispered.

Heart pounding, Darci let her eyes roam the shelves. What exactly was she looking for? she wondered. Something about poisons. She went to Micaela's bookshelves and scanned the spines. The books were all occult titles. She didn't see anything that related to poisons. Except maybe a book on plants. Darci took the book on plants, sat down at Micaela's desk, and began to flip through it.

"Look," she said to Kurt. "She's marked some of these plants—the same ones that are over on the table by the window."

Kurt looked over her shoulder curiously. "They all have really old-fashioned names," he said. "Like something out of Shakespeare—henbane, monkshood, hellebore."

"Maybe I should write them down," Darci said.

Of course, she didn't have any paper. One of Micaela's notebooks lay on top of the desk. Darci reached for it, intending to rip out a page to write on. The notebook fell open to a piece of paper that had been folded inside.

"What's that?" Kurt asked.

Darci unfolded the paper. "It looks like an article from a scientific journal," she said. "It's probably something Micaela got from her parents."

Kurt looked through the notebook as Darci scanned the article.

"It's about Vincent van Gogh," she told him, "and a medical debate that's been going on for years. Doctors are still trying to figure out why van Gogh went insane. There's a part of it that Micaela highlighted. Listen to this.

"'...van Gogh may well have gone mad from digitalis poisoning. At least one of his paintings shows his physician holding a foxglove plant, a source of natural digitalis. From this we can deduce that his doctor prescribed digitalis for him.'"

"So?" Kurt asked.

"So, there's a reproduction of the painting here. And the foxglove—it's one of the plants Micaela's growing over by the window. And there's more.

"'One effect of digitalis poisoning is that the victim often sees yellow halos around light. These golden halos can be clearly seen in many of van Gogh's paintings…'

"Ian just told me he was seeing yellow auras," Darci said excitedly. "Micaela must have given him something made from foxglove."

"Maybe not," Kurt said in a grim tone. He showed Darci one of the pages in the notebook. There in Micaela's precise, curving handwriting were notes on a plant called Hearts of Darkness. "She has this record of the number of seeds planted, soil conditions, and stuff," Kurt explained. "But get this.

"'Administered test dose of 10 milligrams of H/D powder dissolved in 8 oz. juice to D.C. Resulted in nausea, mild convulsions, and 3-hour sleep. Will have to at least double dose for full toxic effect.'"

Darci felt herself shaking. "D.C.," she said. "That's me. Micaela used a test dose on me the first time I came over here. That's why I got so sick! It's all coming together now. The very first day I met her, she bought a poison ring. And today she has lunch with Ian and he winds up in the hospital with convulsions…"

"I wonder whether she gave him the foxglove or the Hearts of Darkness," Kurt said angrily. "Or both."

Darci wasn't about to waste time trying to figure it out. She picked up the phone in Micaela's room and punched in the number for the hospital. "Dr. Bessen, please," she said. "I've got to talk to her. It's an emergency…"

Darci hung up the phone a few minutes later, feeling better than she had all day. "Dr. Bessen says that if it's digitalis poisoning—or even something similar—there's an antidote called Digibind that may work. I think everything's going to be okay."

"I don't think so," Kurt said. He was standing by the window. "Micaela's Acura just pulled up in front of the house. She's here."

CHAPTER 18

Darci felt a cold jolt of panic rip through her. "We've got to get out of here. Before Devon's nanny tells Micaela about Stacey and Jimmy."

"Too late now," Kurt said. "Unless you want to meet Micaela on the stairs." He looked around the room. "We've got to hide."

Darci nodded. She went to the huge wooden wardrobe and opened the doors.

"That's too obvious," Kurt said, starting toward the hallway. "Let's try the next room."

Darci began to follow him, then remembered Micaela's desk. "I'll be there in a second," she said. "I've got to put this stuff back where we found it." She hurried over to the desk, closed the notebook, then returned the book on plants to its place on the shelf.

She took a last glance around. The room

looked fine. Micaela wouldn't be able to tell that anything had been disturbed.

Walking on tiptoe, she made her way to the doorway. She peered down the long, silent hall. There was no way to tell which room Kurt had chosen.

She began to edge out of Micaela's room when she heard it. The sound of someone pounding up the wooden stairway. Darci's heart began to race. She'd waited too long. It was Micaela; she was sure of it. And she'd be here any second.

Too panicked to think, Darci darted back into Micaela's room, shut the door behind her, crouched down onto the floor, and slid beneath the high four-poster bed.

Please don't look under the bed, she prayed silently. *Please don't look under the bed.*

Darci flinched at the sound of the heavy wooden door being flung open. It was definitely Micaela. She could see the familiar black suede boots entering the room slowly, deliberately.

Darci's heart was hammering so loudly, she couldn't believe Micaela didn't hear it. But Micaela didn't look under the bed. She flung open the wardrobe doors and began to search for something in the wardrobe.

Micaela's boots crossed the room again, then

Darci smelled the familiar scent of candles being lit. She heard the sounds of the shades being drawn.

What's she doing? Darci wondered. Maybe Micaela hadn't talked to Devon's nanny. Was it possible that she really didn't know Darci and Kurt were in the house?

Darci waited, head pressed against the floor, trying to be as still as possible. How long would it be before Micaela left the room? What if Micaela stayed in here all night? How long would Kurt wait for her?

"Earth and sky, moon and stars," Micaela began to chant, "fire and wind, energies of the dark, I summon you now. I have done all you asked. Kristin Harper has been given to the darkness. Ian Hassler is no longer an obstacle."

Hearing that Micaela was responsible for Ian's sickness didn't surprise Darci. But what in the world had Micaela done to Kristin?

"Voice that has guided me for so long," Micaela went on, "tell me what I must do next."

Darci listened. The room was absolutely silent.

Then Micaela murmured, "Cut a finger from the dead girl, take earth from her grave, and give these in an offering to the dark. I shall do as you ask."

Darci shut her eyes, sick to her stomach. Micaela had not only murdered and buried Kristin, but now she was going back to the scene of the crime to cut off one of Kristin's fingers for some creepy ritual sacrifice. *God,* Darci thought, *how could I have wanted to be like her?*

She remained still as Micaela opened and shut the wardrobe, snuffed out the candles, and left the room.

Darci counted slowly to ten, then got up from under the bed. She inched over to the door and pressed her ear against it. She could hear Micaela going down the stairs, calling out something to Devon's nanny.

Moving silently, Darci inched into the hall. She almost fainted with relief as she saw Kurt emerge from one of the other rooms. But her heart sank as she went to meet him. How was she going to tell her brother that Micaela had killed the girl he loved?

Instantly she knew what she had to do. "Kurt, Micaela may have had something to do with Kristin's disappearance," she told him. "We've got to follow her."

"There's her car," Darci said, spotting the silver of Micaela's Acura reflected in Kurt's headlights.

"She's pulled off the road. I can't believe she's parked way out here."

Kurt swerved sharply and pulled up behind Micaela's car. Night had fallen. They were in a remote, heavily wooded section of the Catskills. They'd been following Micaela's car for what seemed like hours. Twice, they'd nearly lost her, but each time they managed to find her again, driving farther and farther east.

"She's not in the car anymore," Kurt said, cutting the engine. He leaned across Darci, got a flashlight from the glove compartment, and started to get out. He hesitated. "Maybe you ought to wait for me here," he said.

"Are you crazy?" Darci countered, getting out of the van. "We're in this together."

Kurt shone the flashlight in a circle around them. "Where'd she go?" he wondered. "There's nothing out here except trees and rocks."

"Shine the flashlight over to the left again," Darci said. "I thought I saw something reflected in the light."

"It's a chain," Kurt said. "Between two stone posts."

Darci followed her brother to the chain. His light shone on a rough footpath. "This must lead to something," Darci said.

"It goes up the mountain." Kurt switched off the light.

"Why'd you do that?" Darci asked.

"Because if Micaela is up there, I don't want her to see us," Kurt said. "Try to be quiet." He ducked beneath the chain and started uphill. Darci gave her eyes a few moments to adjust to the darkness, then followed.

Was Micaela really up there? she wondered. And if she was, would they find her uncovering Kristin's grave? Again, Darci debated whether or not she ought to warn Kurt. And once again, she couldn't find the words to tell him that Kristin was dead.

The path grew steeper as they continued, and the trees seemed to close around them. Darci was aware of the strong, wintry scent of the pines, the sound of an owl calling, and dried leaves crunching beneath her feet. And something else—something that made her very uneasy. Darci tried to identify what it was that she sensed—an animal, another person, a spirit of some sort? No, it was the forest itself. There was something wrong with this part of the woods. Something that felt like death.

Ahead of her, Kurt came to a sudden stop. Seconds later Darci saw why. There was Micaela, barefoot and dressed in a long dark cloak, in a clearing about twenty yards away. Her back to them, she stood in the very center of a circle that had been etched into the ground. Moonlight made her hair glow like silver thread against her dark cloak. Micaela seemed to belong to this place, as if she were part of the night itself.

Darci watched breathlessly as Micaela spoke in a ringing voice, calling on the earth and sky, stars and planets, and the elements. Then to Darci's surprise she dropped to her knees. "Darkness, it's you who must help me now. I gave you Kristin as you asked."

Darci saw Kurt tense and she reached out, putting a restraining hand on his arm. Kurt turned to her and Darci shook her head, silently begging him not to interfere. She knew that if they were going to find Kristin, Micaela would have to lead them to her.

"And I will take from her the sacrifice you've demanded," Micaela went on. "I ask you to guide my hand, give me courage—"

Darci never heard the rest of Micaela's words. Something caught her attention—something was moving along the edges of the trees.

A human shape, caked in filth, moving with slow, dragging steps.

No, Darci thought, *it can't be*. She'd heard Micaela say that Kristin was dead. A crazy memory came back to her—Ian talking about Micaela spending Halloween night in the graveyard, trying to raise the dead.

What had Micaela done?

Darci felt herself begin to shake as the grotesque figure stepped into the clearing.

Beside her she heard Kurt's voice, bewildered and disbelieving. "Kristin!"

It was true. Micaela had raised the dead. Beneath the thick coating of dirt and leaves, Darci could make out Kristin's fine features. The dead girl stumbled toward them. And then Darci couldn't stop herself—she screamed as if screaming could somehow wake her from this living nightmare.

CHAPTER 19

Micaela whirled at the sound of Darci's scream. A cold smile lit her face. "Darci and Kurt Callahan," she said calmly. "I couldn't have asked for better company."

"Wh-what did you do to Kristin?" Kurt's voice was shaking.

Micaela barely glanced at the ghoulish figure that was slowly staggering toward them. She reached into her cloak and drew out a knife with a long curved blade.

"Darci, listen to me," she said. "You've asked to learn my secrets. Tonight you will, but first you must prove yourself worthy."

Kurt stared at Micaela in amazement. What was going on here? He felt like shaking his sister. "Darci, what's she talking about?"

But Darci didn't answer him. Her body was

perfectly still, her eyes focused on Micaela.

Kristin—or what had been Kristin—stumbled and fell to the ground. Kurt wanted to go to her, and yet he couldn't. The idea of touching the dead girl made his flesh crawl.

Micaela swept her arm toward the ghoulish figure and her eyes glittered in the moonlight. "That's evil," she told Darci. "Kristin was evil and so she had to die. The bull vanquished the scorpion. Earth triumphed over water. And now evil is fighting to return from the grave, to take our victory and destroy us. If you are truly coming into your Taurus, into the power of the earth, then prove it tonight, Darci. Take this knife and finish the work I began."

"Darce!" Kurt grabbed his sister's arm. He was about to drag her back down the mountain when Darci gave him a look that said *Play along with me.*

Kurt hesitated for a second. Then he dropped Darci's arm. And he prayed that his sister knew what she was doing.

"Take the knife, Darci," Micaela repeated. "It's evil for the dead to try to return to the land of the living. If you are truly the earth's child, you must send Kristin back to the earth, where she now belongs."

Kurt watched horrified as Micaela held the

knife out to Darci, and Darci walked forward, her hand outstretched. His sister was moving as though she were in a trance. What if she really was under Micaela's control? And he'd handed over his own sister to a witch!

"Take the knife, Darci." Micaela's voice was soft now, persuasive. "Overcoming the evil is the final obstacle. Send Kristin back to the grave, and then it will just be you and me and Kurt. A circle of friendship that no one will ever break."

Darci closed her hand around the handle of the knife. Moonlight gleamed along its silver blade. Slowly, Darci turned toward where the monstrous figure of Kristin lay.

"Plunge the knife into her heart." Micaela's whisper carried across the clearing with terrifying clarity. "And then cut off her little finger."

Kurt couldn't stand any more. "Darce, no!" he shouted, running toward her.

But Darci was faster. She whirled on Micaela, and suddenly the knife was at Micaela's throat. "You poisoned Ian," she said in a low, furious voice. "And me before him. What did you do to Kristin? Tell me, Micaela."

Kurt wasn't taking any more chances. He slipped off his belt and rushed Micaela from behind, bringing her to the ground in a flying tackle. While Micaela lay thrashing on the ground, he tied her arms with his belt.

He looked up to see Darci, still holding the knife. "Would you put that damn thing down?" Kurt snapped.

Darci shook her head, her face white with terror.

The ghostly figure of Kristin had gotten to its feet and was stumbling toward them, her arms outstretched.

CHAPTER 20

Terrified, Darci glanced from the monster that was walking toward them to where Micaela lay tied on the ground.

"Kristin's dead," Micaela said. "She's come back from the grave, and neither one of you knows how to handle it. Untie me and I'll send her back. If you don't, she'll walk the earth this way forever."

"What'd you do to her?" Darci asked again.

"I buried her alive," Micaela said without emotion. "The earth had to triumph over water. She had to be given to the darkness."

"So you're going to put a knife in her heart," Darci said, feeling sick.

"Yes," Micaela said impatiently. "And I have to take her finger. The voice has asked for it."

"The voice?" Darci backed away from Micaela

and screamed again as she nearly stumbled into Kristin's ghost. It had to be a ghost. There was no way Kristin could have survived being buried alive.

But Kurt was not so sure. "Sounds like something went wrong with your plan, Micaela," he said. "You might have buried her, but you didn't kill her."

"Don't be an idiot!" Micaela snapped. "Free me and I'll send her back to the darkness. Please, it's the best thing for all of us."

"Us?" Kurt's voice was shaking with fury. "What is wrong with you?"

To Darci's astonishment, a tear slid down Micaela's cheek. "Kurt, you've got to listen," she said in a trembling voice. "I gave Kristin to the darkness because she was getting in the way of you and me and Darci. No one can love you the way I can. Kristin was stopping that. She was an obstacle. I couldn't let her get in the way. I had to remove her. Please, Kurt, you have to understand—I did it for you and me and Darci. So we could be together forever."

Kurt gave Micaela a contemptuous look and slowly walked toward the ghostly figure of Kristin.

"She's dead, Kurt," Micaela screamed. "You can't have her any more!"

"Kris—is that you?" he asked.

Kristin nodded. She tried to speak but only a hoarse gasp came out.

"Darce, do me a favor and make sure that Micaela doesn't go anywhere," Kurt said.

Darci nodded, fighting her own tears.

Her brother was still facing Kristin. He was gazing at her as if she were dressed in a beautiful prom gown—not covered with mud.

"It's okay," Kurt said in a gentle voice as Kristin collapsed in his arms. He brushed the dirt from her face and kissed her. "It's all over now."

Check your horoscope for December—
Zodiac Chiller #5 is on its way!

Linda's cruise to disaster…

NEVER LOVE A LIBRA

"There's no way Billy could have survived the shark attack. He's dead, Linda. Dead."

The words echoed in Linda's ear as she stumbled back to her cabin, her wet clothes clinging to her body. Maybe a hot shower would take her mind off this terrible night. A nice long shower, long enough to forget Billy Jackson—forever.

About ten feet from her cabin door, Linda noticed the bloody spot on the carpet.

A bloody trail. She started to tremble.

No! a voice screamed inside her head.

But the trail of blood could only mean one thing: Billy Jackson was alive.

ELLEN STEIBER

Ellen Steiber was born on the cusp of Aries and Taurus. She is the author of over twenty-five books for young readers, including *Tales of the Gross and Gruesome*. Although she used to be an editor and live in New York City, it was in her stars to move to the Southwest. So she moved to Tucson, Arizona, where she now writes books and can actually see the stars. There she shares a house in the desert with a good friend and three cats. Her youngest cat, Arizona, is a Taurus and has asked Ellen to assure you that not all Taureans are twisted.

YOU COULD RECEIVE A COOL ASTRO-PENDANT!

We hope you enjoyed *Twisted Taurus*. Be sure to read all the upcoming books in this exciting new series, available wherever books are sold!

Your opinion is important to us, and we'd love to hear from you. If you are one of the first 1,000 readers to return this questionnaire, we will send you an awesome moon-and-star necklace!

1. What is your astrological sign?

2. Do you check your horoscope
   __ Every day
   __ Once a week
   __ Once a month
   __ Rarely
   __ Never

3. I thought *Twisted Taurus* was
   __ Celestial
   __ Good but not stellar
   __ Less than earth-shattering
   __ Death Star

4. Have you read any other Zodiac Chillers?
   __ Yes   __ No

5. If so, which titles?
   __ *Rage of Aquarius*
   __ *The Scorpio Society*
   __ *In Leo's Lair*

6. Do you read any other horror series?
   __ Yes   __ No

7. If so, which ones?

8. Where did you purchase this book?
   __ Bookstore   __ Drugstore   __ Supermarket
   __ Library   __ Book club   __ Book fair

Please send this completed questionnaire to:
Zodiac Chillers Editor
Random House, Inc.
201 East 50th Street—28th Floor
New York, NY 10022

Offer valid through December 31, 1995.
Please allow 6 weeks for delivery of your astro-pendant.

Thanks, and happy reading!